My Fire

My Heart

Alexandra Larson

ISBN: 979-8-9874887-7-5 (paperback)
ISBN: 979-8-9874887-6-8 (e-book)

100% Author Written
100% Author Designed Cover (Photos licensed from DepositPhotos)

First Edition: December 2024

Author Note

This novella is a collection of interconnected vignettes that fills in the sweet and spicy moments of Sloane & Nico's love story. The external plot from Books 1-3 is glossed over or only mentioned in passing. It is not a novel-paced story and should *not* be read as a standalone.

If you are a fan of tandem rereads, I've included the book and chapter you should read up to before switching back to the novella.

This novella includes descriptions of kidnapping, burning, trauma, PTSD flashbacks, and sexually explicit (dragon shifter) content. There are discussions of (but not descriptions of) a character being tortured as a prisoner of war.

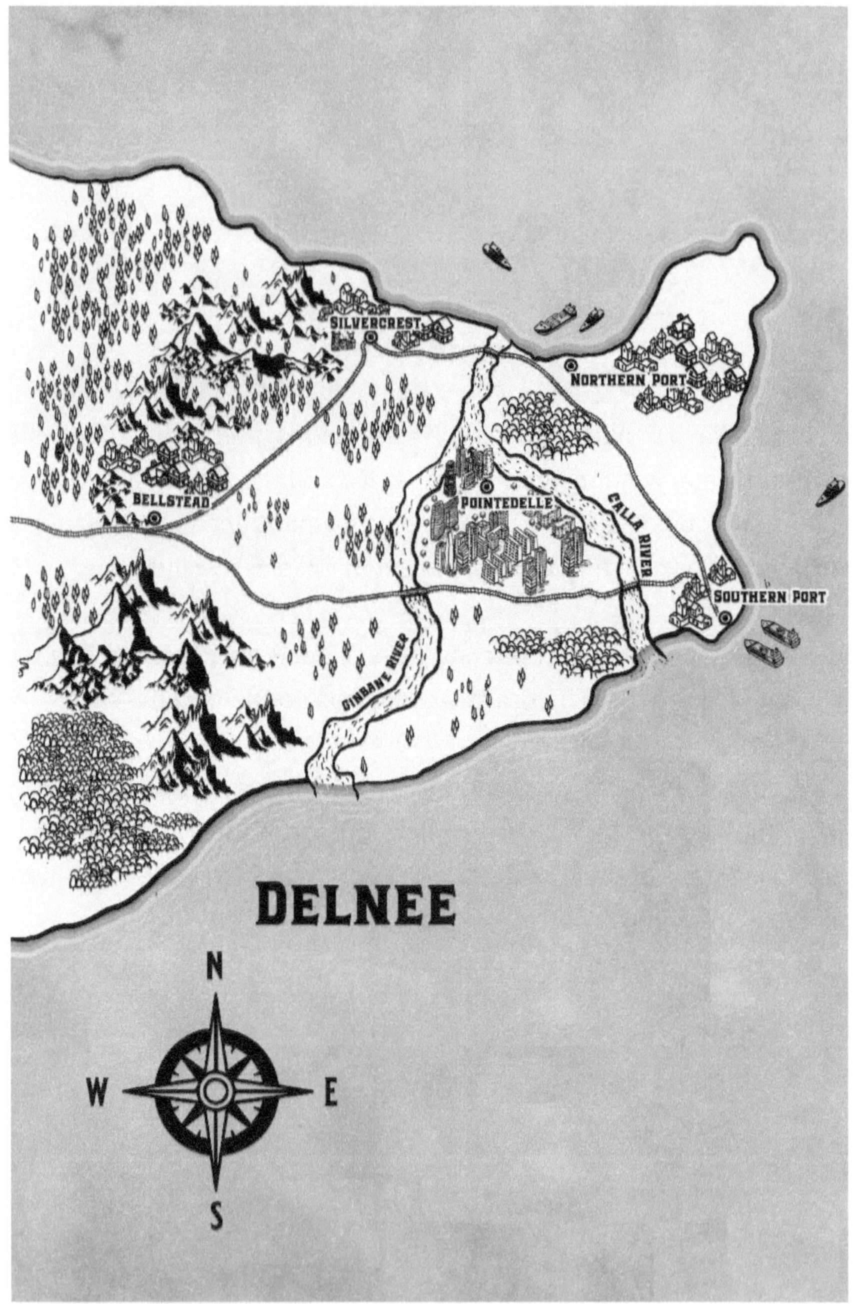

Silvercrest
Northern Port
Bellstead
Pointedelle
Calla River
Dinbane River
Southern Port
DELNEE
N
W
E
S

FAE PRISON
THE HOLLOW
MOLBRIDGE
WILLOW LAKE
PALAGUI CITY
PORT HAZELLE
MERBANY
CORAL BEACH

PALAGUI

Chapter One: The Hopeless Romantic

Tandem Read to Ascend from the Shadows Chapter 20
Sloane

"Seriously? You're baking your infatuation cookies already? You just met the guy."

Gwen strolled into the kitchen of our shared penthouse apartment. Her pursed lips didn't put a dent in my bubbly vibes. I smiled, used my elbow to push back my short blonde hair, and patted my flour-caked hands on my apron.

"I have no idea what you're talking about," I replied in a sing-song voice to the cadence of the music that was blaring through the stereo system. I danced and bumped my hip into hers as the song hit the chorus.

Gwen curled her lip and shoved my arm with her usual morning grumble. Her ash-brown hair was haphazardly pulled back, and she was still wearing makeup from last night on her warm brown skin. I thought she'd be in a better mood since she finally took Rae home last night.

Granted...the circumstances had been less than ideal since Rae was passed out from a draxis attack.

But *still*. I was pretty sure I heard some smooching coming from her bedroom earlier.

Gwen slumped onto the stool on the opposite side of the island.

"I don't know why you call them that," I said, slapping her hand before she could grab a cookie from the cooling rack. "I bake all the time. Not just when…" I wrinkled my nose, thinking of the right way to describe it. "When I meet someone that I might, possibly, sort of, think I could have feelings for."

Gwen rolled her eyes. "You met him last night. Cool yourself."

I waggled my eyebrows. "Am I the only one baking infatuation cookies this morning?"

She ignored my question while pouring herself a cup of black coffee. I assumed I wasn't going to get an answer until she finally said, "Rae was traumatized last night despite her mind being wiped. It would have been highly inappropriate to make a move on her."

"Uh huh," I said in a feigned serious tone, my hands on my hips. "Highly inappropriate, Gwen Nueblots. I'm so disappointed in you."

She scarfed a cookie. "Your impression of my mother is really improving."

"So," I said, elongating the word.

Gwen mumbled something with her mouth full of cookie.

"What was that?" I leaned over the counter and kicked one foot up.

"I kissed her."

I jumped up and down, squealing, and Gwen scrunched up her face at the high-pitched noise.

"It was a goodbye kiss, okay? She was confused about why she slept over if we didn't…you know, do anything. I told her I really liked her but wanted to take it slow, and then *she* asked for a kiss."

I clapped my hands. "Yay!"

Gwen looked down into her coffee; the corners of her mouth twitched, cracking her grumpy mask.

I pretended my spatula was my microphone and started singing along to the fun, poppy love song that was playing. When the chorus came in, I thrust my hand forward to aim my spatula/microphone at Gwen's mouth.

She leaned forward and deadpanned the chorus at the same time that I sang at the top of my lungs, "I just wanna love yoooou."

My phone rang and interrupted the song. "It's Amaya."

I put her on speaker, and the three of us spent the next twenty minutes discussing, in graphic detail, her night with Rien.

"She sounds happy," I said after hanging up with her.

"She does," Gwen said, voice brittle.

"What?" I asked. "Are you worried Rien will tell the government she's a high priestess?"

"No, I was just thinking…" She broke off a piece of cookie, crumbs flying all over the counter.

"It's only a matter of time before Rien and Amaya start actually dating."

"Yep!" I said, icing the cookies. "Why's that bad?"

"It's not. I'm just wondering if you really want to be in a relationship with August?"

I scrunched up my brows. "Well, I don't know. Like you said, I just met him."

"Yeah," Gwen said. "And we both know it can never go anywhere."

I chewed on my lip. She wasn't wrong.

I loved love. I wanted to find *the one*. To be swept off my feet in a grand romance.

But I wouldn't get a say in deciding who I would build a life with.

It'd always been my dream to have a big family. My parents died when I was eight years old, and I didn't have brothers or sisters, just my grandmother, and Gwen, of course. When we were little, we liked to pretend we were Delnee's best field agents: saving the world, one mission at a time. A childhood attempt to rewrite the past into a timeline where I could save my parents from the mission they'd been forced to complete.

I knew realistically, in a couple of decades, I'd have to accept my fate. The High Priestess Society chose what job we had, what missions we went on, and the person we'd marry.

"If you date Rien's friend and then dump him, it's going to make it awkward for everyone." Gwen pursed her lips. "And I'm going to have to feel everyone's emotions when it blows up."

I sighed.

"If you really like him, go for it. I support you, but..." Gwen said. "If it's just a fling, maybe find someone who isn't going to make our friend group an emotional minefield?"

I bobbed my head absently, focusing on icing my last cookie. "You're probably right."

"Sorry," Gwen said, giving me a sympathetic look, or rather empathetic look, since I hadn't been shielding my emotions and she could feel my disappointment.

"No. You *are* right," I said, shaking my arms out to dispel the lingering moroseness. It wasn't fair to subject Gwen to my disappointment. And it wouldn't be fair to Amaya if I made things awkward for our friend group.

I picked up my phone and started texting August my usual *it's not you, it's me* text. "I don't think we should mention this to Amaya. She'll be upset."

Gwen nodded and changed the subject.

Chapter Two: The Free Spirit

Nico

"I just wanna love yooou," I belted out and launched myself in the air to do a jump kick.

My shoulder-length auburn hair fell out of its bun as I landed on the stage with a loud *crunch*.

"NICO!" Daria's voice echoed through the bar as the last boom of the bass hit and the room went quiet.

I cringed and stepped out of the hole I'd created in the stage. Replacing the microphone on the stand, I yelled, "I'll fix it, Daria!"

She put a hand on her hip and gave me a peeved expression.

I tried to dazzle her with my widest smile as I sprinted down the hall to the back office, grabbed what I was looking for, and returned.

"See?" I said and carefully positioned the yellow caution fold-out stand—the one used when the floor is wet—over the hole. "Problem solved."

The crowd burst into riotous laughter, and I grinned.

Daria was not amused. "Out." She pointed to the door, and my shoulders crumpled.

The crowd booed, but Daria waved a hand. "You all are next," she warned. "If you don't like it, then leave my bar. Or I could cancel karaoke night altogether?"

That shut everyone up. No one left. They wouldn't leave. Everyone loved Daria. They liked me for my antics, but even I could admit I took it a little too far this time.

"How was I supposed to know your stage couldn't handle a little jump kick?" I asked Daria, passing her on the way to the door.

"You would think being built like a heavyweight champion, you'd realize your own strength," Daria said as she delivered drinks to a table.

"I'm built like a heavyweight champion because I *was* one." A long time ago, but I still had my boxing muscles. They were just shielded by a layer of fluff nowadays, the perils of taste-testing my own baking.

"My point exactly," Daria said, smiling. She swatted me with the white towel on her shoulder, and I knew we were fine. She had to kick me out so no one else would get any ideas about destroying her bar.

I winked at her. "You know I can be very gentle if you like it that way, Daria."

She rolled her eyes. Her short black hair waving around as she zipped off toward the bar. "You're going to pay me back for those repairs."

"Put it on my tab!" I held the door open with one hand and turned to shout my final goodbye. "Farewell patrons of The Cave. You've been a great crowd!"

The cheering hushed as I stepped out onto the sidewalk.

I put my hands on my hips and looked down the street, contemplating my next moves. It was still early. The sun had barely set, and I wasn't ready to go home, but I didn't know what—

"Nico!"

I turned and opened my arms to both my sides. "Stella! Good. You're coming with me? Where should we go next?"

Stella glared, pushing a piece of brown hair from her eyes. She looked a little rumpled, like she had to push through the crowd to get out. "You just left me."

"I got kicked out."

"Well, yeah, but you could have grabbed me."

I scratched the back of my neck. It hadn't occurred to me. "I didn't think you'd want to leave."

As she took a deep breath, her chest rose, pushing her cleavage into my sightline. She started saying something, but I got a little distracted by staring, only tuning back in when my mind registered the words I'd heard my entire life.

"You're too much. This isn't working," she said.

I refocused on her face. "What?" I tried to smile. "Stella, come on. Daria isn't actually mad. I went a little overboard, but—"

She shook her head and crossed her arms. "It's not just that. This is one of the many things you do. You aren't sixteen and neither am I. I want someone I can plan a future with."

I started fidgeting, shaking out my hands. "You said you didn't want a stuck-up, serious guy. I thought we were having fun."

"We were. We did. You're an awesome friend, Nico," she said, her tone almost pitying.

I winced.

"But I want a life partner," she continued. "Someone who's going in the same direction as me, but I don't think you even know which direction is up."

I pointed to the sky.

She pressed her lips together. "We don't work."

I put my hand down and stared at my shoes. "Yeah. Okay."

It was fine. I wasn't heartbroken. We'd only been going out for a few weeks. It just stung that no matter how hard I tried to get my shit together, everyone eventually found out the truth.

I was too much.

Too much energy. Too chatty. Too disorganized. Too scatterbrained. Too carefree. Too *go with the flow*.

They all jived with it at first. I'd always been able to get along with people, but eventually the girls I dated got annoyed that I didn't have more ambition. That I was satisfied being a fae power trainer for high school kids. That I didn't want to move out of my best friend's garage apartment.

I dated a lot, I mean *a lot*, but I never had a long-term girlfriend.

"Can we still be friends?" Stella asked.

"Of course." I forced a smile and wrapped an arm around her shoulders, pulling her in for a side hug. "Can I call you a car?"

She nodded. "Thanks, Nico. You really are the best."

Irrational annoyance flared, lashing at my chest like the whip of my inner dragon's tail as I tapped through my car share app.

"Anytime," I gritted out.

Chapter Three: The Flames

Tandem Read to Ascend from the Shadows Chapter 25
Sloane

Tension spread through my body as I walked home from work. I replayed my interactions with the leaders of the High Priestess Society over and over, trying to figure out why I was being dismissed. Amaya had figured out the draxis attack patterns, and I'd brought the evidence to the Society, but they weren't using the information to stop them.

Self-righteous anger distracted me, so I faltered as an arm curled around my waist and hauled me backward. A black hood went over my head. Recovering from my hesitation, I slammed my elbow into the stomach of my attacker. He grunted, but flames burned my arms.

I opened my mouth to scream, only for fire to engulf me.

The repulsive, acrid smell of burning flesh filled my nose. Heat melted my organs. There was no fighting—no escaping—the blistering hot agony that tore through my body.

The sound of squealing tires was the last thing I heard before my vision whited out.

I woke with a cloth covering my eyes and zip ties binding my wrists, but there was no pain. My wounds had been healed by my power while I was unconscious.

"You make a single move, and I'll burn you again," a deep masculine voice warned.

I didn't heed his warning the first time. I thrashed and threw myself around, trying to break free, fighting the solisers blindfolded inside the back of a van.

But I was outnumbered.

They didn't give me a second warning. They trapped me in an infernal existence, burning me until I passed out, and upon waking, they burned me again.

Each time my consciousness returned, I tried to keep my breathing even, tried to feign sleep. For a few minutes, I'd escape detection. I'd inhale air that didn't choke me with smoke. I'd hear sounds that weren't my own screams. But too soon, they'd realize I was awake, and they'd begin the agonizing cycle over.

Each time was worse than the last.

Even though I'd healed, my nerve endings, my body's intelligence, remembered every torturous moment of living within the flames. My skin returned to its same complexion, but my veins and my heart and my soul remained charred.

On the outside, I looked fine.

But inside, pieces of me burned away; ash curled into the air, leaving me with a body that was no longer whole. I'd shriveled up into someone I couldn't recognize anymore.

Chapter Four: The Irony

Nico

I answered my phone on the second ring. Bash didn't bother with a greeting. "Where are you? Can you come home?" He sounded out of breath.

"Yeah," I said, twirling my car keys around my finger as I walked through the school parking lot. "I'm leaving work. Had to stay late. What's wrong?"

He didn't answer.

Shadows materialized in front of me. A hand grabbed my shoulder, and my best friend sifted us into the living room of the townhouse.

"What the hell? You know you're gonna have to sift me back to my car, right?" I furrowed my brows and took a good look at him.

Bash's blue eyes were frantic, and his normally pristine attire was scorched and torn, though I couldn't see any wounds. He was bleeding shadows; they hung thick around his shoulders and around his hands.

"What happened to you?"

He raked a hand through his black hair, the long portion on the top matted with blood. "I'm fine. I was healed. Got into a fight with some solisers."

"How? There are no solisers in Delnee?"

"It's a long story."

He started pacing the length of the room, and I plopped onto the couch. He wasn't moving like he was hurt, so I wasn't too concerned for his wellbeing. His shadow had probably taken over and gotten him into a fight.

It wouldn't have been the first time.

I propped my legs on the coffee table, waiting for him to gather his thoughts.

He halted and turned to me. "She's my mate."

My jaw dropped, and my legs fell from the coffee table as I leaned forward. Bash had never pulled a prank on me before, but that's what this was, right?

Right?

Mates were rare. I wasn't entirely convinced they even existed.

I stood up. "You fucking with me?"

He shook his head, eyes wide and serious. "The girl I told you about? The one sticking her nose into the draxis stuff? She's my mate."

I rubbed a hand across my mouth and put the other on my hip. "You're sure? How do you know?"

He nodded and resumed his pacing. "Every time we touch, our powers react. She's a darkyra and a high priestess. Shadows and light. She—"

He rubbed at a spot below his collarbone. "My heart aches when she's near. My shadow has been uncontrollable since I met her. He's busting out every time I'm near her. I don't know what to do. One of these days, I'm not going to be able to catch him."

I sank to the couch, dazed. "Okay. Okay. Well, this isn't a problem."

If anyone deserved someone who loved him unconditionally, it was Bash.

Well, someone other than me.

Someone who could give him the relationship I couldn't.

It was really too bad that sexuality wasn't a choice.

I shook my head, annoyed that I was losing focus. Again.

Gathering my hair, I twisted it into a low bun. "You have a mate. That's amazing, Bash. Did you get into a fight defending her honor or something? That had to be a panty dropper."

He gave me a horrified look. "I haven't gotten to the worst part."

I sighed. My best friend was going to give me the same monologue he always did when I tried to encourage him to date. He was too busy running the country. He had to focus on saving Adriana. His shadow would hurt them.

I opened my mouth to outline my counter arguments, but he shut me up before I could get them out.

"I'm pretty sure one of her friends was taken to the research center," he said. "Solisers took her, tried to take my mate and her other friend too. That's the fight I was in."

I snapped my mouth shut.

Shadow Bash went to the research center every so often when there was a new shipment of high priestesses and took their powers to keep the queen, and Palagui, alive.

"Yeah. Maybe don't take your mate's friend's powers, then?"

Bash rolled his eyes. "Thanks for the advice."

"It's alright, okay? We'll get her out. I know I can get blueprints of the building."

"I don't know for sure if that's where she is yet. I need to track her down, but even so, we are *not* going to break in. I'll ask Xenos at the next council meeting to release her."

"Right," I said. "And after you try that, and it fails, I'll have the blueprints and a plan that'll actually work."

With his back toward me, he stared out the window. "That won't be necessary..." he trailed off, voice cracking. His posture stiffened.

A cold slither of dread wound its way around my spine.

Shadows curled around him like a heavy blanket. He bent his neck left and right, and then clasped his hands behind his back.

When he turned around, his void eyes stared back at me. Shadows darkened his blue irises and took over the whites of his eyes.

"I've been unable to use my power the entire time I was in Delnee. I need to use it now," he said in the deeper voice of his shadow.

I forced myself not to react, only nodding at Shadow Bash's excuse.

It wasn't a bad excuse. Fae became sick when we couldn't use our powers, and Bash had been in Delnee all summer, so it was plausible.

Shadow Bash probably thought he was so clever giving me that line. Or he thought I was an idiot who couldn't tell when my best friend wasn't in control of his body.

Probably both.

"Sure thing, bud." I got up from the couch and made my way toward the kitchen. "I'll go get dinner started."

"Wait," Shadow Bash said.

I halted. I needed to get my shock stick. "Yeah?"

"I need you to make fake identification for my female. I'm bringing her to Palagui."

"Are you?" I asked.

He nodded once. "She will be mine."

"Uh huh," I said. "And does she know this?" I couldn't help goading him. This bastard was the reason the real Bash wouldn't let anyone get close to him.

"She may not recognize our connection yet, but she will." A maniacal grin filled his face. "Together, we will be the most powerful fae in all of Palagui. In the world, perhaps."

I suppressed my shudder. "Perhaps," I mocked. "Well, I'll go do that."

He didn't follow me at first, lost in whatever sick world domination fantasy he was having, but before I could sneak out the back door to my apartment, he reappeared and kept a close eye on me all night. I made us dinner and faked conversation so he wouldn't know that I knew he wasn't *my* Bash.

He didn't let me get my laptop either. He sifted to my apartment and grabbed it for me, claiming he was just very eager to get the paperwork done.

I worked for hours on the fake identification for his mate. I didn't know if the real Bash wanted this, but it kept the ruse going.

It was late when I finished. I told him I was going to bed, but instead retrieved my shock stick, snuck back inside, and blasted him with it from behind. I wasn't quick enough to catch his fall, and he tumbled hard onto the floor.

I stared down at my best friend. "What a mess. I hope this girl is worth it."

I crouched down, picked him up, and laid him on the couch, before settling in the chair opposite him.

Who was I kidding? Of course, this girl would be worth it. His mate? The perfect match for him? Fae would do anything to find their mate.

While I waited for Bash to wake up, I grabbed one of the anatomy books that my healer, Karina, had given me after my healing ritual. I really couldn't sit still to read an entire book, let alone one that was as dry as a textbook, but I knew we were going to need information on magical biology.

By the time Bash finally opened his eyes—no shadows haunting his irises anymore—I'd only managed to get through one chapter, but it was the most important chapter.

"Since when do you read?" he asked, wincing and rubbing his arm where he fell as he sat up.

"Since you went and got yourself a mate," I said. "Figured we'd need to know what we were up against."

Fury lit his eyes, and for a second, I wondered if Shadow Bash actually woke up. "Up against? You will not harm her."

I held up my hands in surrender. "Calm down. I meant to better understand mate stuff. Goddess, don't get so worked up."

He rubbed his eyes and slumped over. "Sorry. I just...Fuck. I'm tired."

"Shadow Bash took over."

He sighed. "Thanks for getting me back. The stress is making me sloppy."

"I made Amaya identification so you could bring her here," I said, wanting to give him something to take away the heaviness that was weighing him down.

He hummed absently and held his head in his hands.

"You should probably wear cuffs around her," I continued. "The longer you're around each other, the more your auras will intertwine. Your powers will keep increasing."

"Who knows if the cuffs are even enough," he said. "I probably shouldn't be around her at all."

"Well, just don't fuck her," I said. "You'll get a bigger boost."

His head snapped up. "Don't talk about her like that," he growled.

I snorted and tossed the book onto his lap. "You've got it bad. You weren't even this possessive of Jeremy. I can't wait to meet her."

Sebastian stared at the book, took a deep breath, and exhaled it out slow. "You won't be meeting her. I can't risk my shadow growing more powerful. I can't risk him hurting her."

"According to that book, your shadow won't be capable of hurting her. Well, after you fuc—I mean, after you make sweet, sweet love to her, neither of you will be capable of killing the other. Your powers and auras will be intertwined, which will prevent it."

Bash shook his head. "We don't know that for sure. It doesn't matter what this anatomy book says. There's no research on mates who have had power as strong as mine. And if she's my mate, her shadow is just as strong."

I crossed my arms over my chest and leaned back. He'd cave. I knew he'd cave, but there would be no telling him that now. "Okay."

"I'll get her friend out of the research center, and then I'll leave her alone. I don't need to be in Delnee anymore, so I'll put an ocean between us."

"Right."

He got a vacant look in his eye, staring at the wall behind me. His body deflated.

"You know," I started. "If you really want to get your shadow under control, you could try that program I told you about."

"I don't have time for that. Therapy can't fix what's wrong with me, Nico," he said, waving a dismissive hand.

I sighed because that was always his response. "Alright."

"Can you tell your father I need his support at the council meeting?"

"Yeah. How much do you want me to tell him?"

"Only what he needs to know. I don't want anyone to know about Amaya being my mate."

I nodded. "I'll get started on a Plan B too, in case Xenos isn't in a giving mood."

He never was.

"That's not necessary," Bash said, standing, his shadows gathering. "I'll be home in a few days."

"With your mate," I teased him.

"No. Alone."

"Uh huh," I said as he sifted and disappeared. I shook my head. The next time I saw my best friend—his mate would be with him.

I just knew it.

Chapter Five: The Dragon

Tandem Read to Descend into the Void Chapter 8
Sloane

I was locked in a prison tower, surrounded by fire. My mind and body were paralyzed, burning in the flames of hell.

"Sloane, are you okay?"

"What happened after you were kidnapped?"

"What's the last thing you remember?"

"Nico, what's wrong?"

But then, the dragon extinguished the pain.

"You've got to be fucking kidding me," a male voice whispered.

Calloused palms engulfed mine, warmth seeping into me. "I'm going to get you out of here, okay?" the dragon said.

I blinked and took in the sight of a kneeling male. His features were distorted by my tears, but the orange scales trailing up his neck were undeniable. He glowed; his soft, protective haze covered me.

"Okay," I croaked.

"Plan B?" someone asked.

"Fuck any plans," the dragon replied while holding my gaze. "I'm going to murder everyone in this fucking building and watch it burn to the ground." He pushed a piece of hair off my face. His fingers were hot against the shell of my ear, and yet, I still shivered as they skimmed down my neck.

My eyes were closing, his touch making me sleepy.

I jumped as a knock on the door startled me from my dragon's protective cocoon.

"Time's up."

And my dragon was gone.

Come back. Please come back, my heart cried out.

People talked, but I didn't register anything. I braced myself for the flames. That had been the pattern: if I found a moment of relief, the pain would come next.

The dragon reappeared before the next round of my torture could begin.

"Can I carry you?" he asked. There was blood on his face, and I had the urge to wipe it away, but I wasn't sure if I could move. My limbs were heavy, muscles dried out and crunchy. My magic must have been burned away. Somehow, I managed to nod.

He gathered me in his arms, and I basked in his warmth, pressing my face into his chest, my nose into the crook of his neck. He smelled so good, like sweet dark berries and a slight smoky musk. A berry mountain pie cooked over a fire.

It made me nostalgic for something I'd never experienced. Like my soul was coming home to somewhere my body had never been.

I ran my hands along his neck and down his chest. The golden-orange scales had multiplied; they peeked out from under his collar and climbed his neck, covering the strong cut of his jaw. Spiked horns protruded from the handsome male's auburn hair. A tapered tail flicked my calf.

I grabbed Amaya's arm as she walked by. "Amaya, a dragon has come to save me. To break me out of my prison tower. Isn't that romantic?"

Just like the fairy tales. The grand romance I'd always wanted.

"Yeah, Sloane. It is," Amaya said, but her voice was distant. "You have to be super quiet now though, okay? So the dragon can get you out."

"Okay," I said sleepily and closed my eyes, snuggling into my dragon's arms.

Oranges and reds and golds filled my vision. I should have been afraid—dragons made fire—but his glow was made up of crystallized fragments of love, mirrored and refracted against one another, growing exponentially behind my eyelids. Peace filled the dark, ashy crevices that had been carved out of my heart.

I couldn't be afraid of the flames when my dragon controlled them.

Chapter Six: The Bargain

Tandem Read to Descend into the Void Chapter 9
Nico

The flames of my power had raged in my core as I walked across the threshold of the research center. I'd written it off as nerves. My usual chaotic energy revving up.

And then I saw her.

My inner dragon perked up. Not even the threat of getting knocked out in the boxing ring could make my scattered thoughts focus like they had in that moment.

My heart pounded, ached, *burned* for her.

The fire in my veins blazed, threatening to consume my entire being, melt away who I was and remake me into *hers*.

The pain spread to encompass my entire body. The pulse of the ache only released me when I kneeled before the source of the fire in my heart and touched her skin.

She was cold. Too cold. Her eyes were glassy and lost. She was sick. The marks on her inner elbows, at the top of her high priestess initiation tattoo, made me want to roar, made the beast inside of me rage against its shackles. The seven phases of the moon were distorted by puckered red skin. The suppression crap the research center shot her full of was eating her away.

I hadn't wanted to shift like this…in…well, ever. Sharp talons clawed at me from under my skin, my power trying to turn me inside out. The ghost of my dragon form hovered outside my body, waiting for me to fill in the outline with my shape.

Even the wards around the research center wouldn't have held me back if I decided to burn the place down.

But revenge would need to wait. She needed me. That simple fact cooled my dragon's rage enough that I could focus on getting her out.

When Sloane reached out to Amaya and admitted to seeing my true form, it confirmed what I was feeling.

"A dragon has come to save me."

The ache in my heart.

The restlessness of my dragon.

The flames flickering to life in the core of my power.

It all meant only one thing.

If her vision could pierce through the fae skin I wore and see who I truly was…

She was my mate.

Keep your cool. Don't tell anyone, Bash said in my head. The threat underlying his words was clear. He knew better than anyone the transformation I was currently undergoing.

The same one that had overcome him. The one that had made it impossible for him to leave Amaya in Delnee.

I nodded once, but barely looked at him before following Gwen down the hall. She'd already incapacitated the guard outside the rear of the research center when I stepped out with my mate in my arms.

We pressed our backs to the wall and waited for Daria's signal that the coast was clear to run to the car.

"If you think this knight in shining armor act is going to work to get into her pants, you're wrong," Gwen hissed. "Once she is safe, I'm not letting you anywhere near her."

I couldn't help the rumbling growl that rose in my chest. Gwen's eyes widened. I knew she was seeing the orange ring of my power outlining my irises.

I had to fight the urge to shift and fly away with Sloane, hide her and keep her to myself. A dragon hoarding its treasure. My greatest treasure.

Maybe I would have too, if Sloane hadn't reached up and pressed her palm over my aching heart. Her thumb moved back and forth in a soft caress.

"Her bark is worse than her bite," she whispered.

Gwen harrumphed. "You keep quiet. I'm trying to rescue your ass."

A dazed smile played out on Sloane's face. "Then maybe you shouldn't be threatening the male carrying me. I have a feeling his bite is worse than his bark."

"I'd never hurt you," I said.

Her eyes met mine. "I know."

My heart sang, and my dragon preened that our mate already had such a steady belief in our intentions.

"Where are they?" Gwen asked, peeking around the corner. "Do you think they got caught? Do we have another plan to get out of here?"

Yeah. I was going to fly away.

But I didn't think Gwen would approve of that, so I kept my mouth shut and stared at my mate.

She had short blonde hair and a cute upturned nose. Her big green eyes were outlined by the soft flutter of long eyelashes. She struck me utterly speechless. How could anyone be so perfect?

Her eyes drifted halfway closed, and she moved her hand from my heart to grab my neck and pressed her cheek to my chest. "I'm so cold, but you feel nice."

"I'll keep you warm," I promised.

She nuzzled closer.

She was concerningly cold. Solisers naturally had a higher body temperature, but this was something worse.

She murmured something unintelligible, and her head lulled back, passing out.

"Sloane?" I asked, panicked. "Sloane?"

Gwen whipped back around. "What's wrong with her?"

Before I could answer, a car door slammed shut. Gwen ran to the corner of the building to check for Daria's signal.

"Come on! It's clear," she yelled, waving her hand.

I squeezed Sloane tighter so her head and neck didn't jostle as I sprinted to the car. Gwen opened the door to the backseat, and I slid in, not bothering to move Sloane from my lap. I held her, trying to cover as much of her skin with mine, hoping the heat and friction would wake her.

Daria barked a command at Gwen, who tried to get into the back with us, but she relented in whatever fight Daria was having with her and sat in the passenger seat instead.

Gwen turned to look at Sloane. "Why did she pass out?"

"It's probably the suppression they gave her," I said. "It disconnects fae from our powers."

I would know. It was the same shit they gave us as prisoners of war.

Gwen's eyes widened in horror.

"She'll sleep it off and be okay," I added. At least, I hoped.

"Where are they?" Daria muttered, looking toward the entrance.

I repositioned Sloane on my lap and cupped her cheeks, trying to infuse warmth into her cold face.

The door opened, and Sebastian and Amaya climbed in. Daria peeled out of the driveway. I pressed my fingers to the pulse on Sloane's neck and let the steady thrum of her heartbeat be my solace.

"How is she?" Amaya asked.

My eyes didn't leave Sloane's face. "She's alive."

The rest of the car ride was impossibly long. Amaya fell asleep on Bash's shoulder. Gwen and Daria bickered in low voices in the front.

Sloane didn't wake up, but I kept checking her pulse to reassure myself she was alive.

Bash and I talked the entire car ride.

Or rather *he* talked *at me*, since I couldn't send thoughts like he could.

You can't tell her.

I know.

If you tell her, she will tell Amaya, and then Amaya will figure it out.

I know.

They already noticed that you're acting weird. You can't get all possessive over her.

This time I met his gaze and flared my nostrils. If he told me I couldn't see her—I didn't care that he was my best friend—I'd rip his head off.

It's surging, but it will pass, he said. His eyes became pleading. *Please, Nico. I know what you're feeling. I know.* The last "I know" was made up of two lost and broken syllables. It cracked through my single-minded focus.

He was right. My body and mind and life force were realigning because I'd found my mate, but this overwhelming sensation would pass.

I took a deep breath and nodded.

He relaxed, and his gaze fell to the sleeping female on his shoulder. The corners of his eyes pulled down in a helpless, brokenhearted expression.

I swallowed. Sloane was my mate. And there was nothing that would stand in the way of us being together.

But Bash?

He was already juggling Xenos and the country and the queen's health. Not to mention his plans for Adriana. I didn't think his shadow would hurt Amaya, but there was a huge risk that if their relationship escalated, his power would increase.

Shadow Bash didn't need more power. That was for sure.

So Bash couldn't be with his mate.

But I could be with Sloane. I had hope for the future. While he had none.

If he wanted to keep this quiet until we could sort everything out, then I could keep the secret for now.

I looked at Sloane's peaceful, pretty face. She'd been through enough in the past few days. The last thing she needed was to wake up to a male hovering above her, claiming her as her mate, wanting a relationship with her.

Being *too much*.

She needed time to heal. She needed a friendly face, not a possessive dragon circling his treasure like she was an object instead of a person.

***

That thought seemed reasonable for a few hours, but I couldn't bring myself to leave Sloane's side. I'd fallen asleep in a chair beside her bed, and a hand on my shoulder shook me awake.

Bash glared at me. He tilted his head to the door and wordlessly walked out.

I glanced at Sloane and pulled her covers up a little, fixing them for Gwen too, who slept next to her, and then crept out of the room.

"Is Amaya okay?" I asked as I entered his bedroom. His back was to me, standing in front of the bar cart.

"She exhausted her power. We both did, but she's fine," he said, pouring scotch into a glass and handing it to me.

"Good," I said, taking a sip.

He poured his own and turned to face me, his face blank with stern authority. "I want you to make a bargain with me."

I downed the rest of my drink. "We're best friends, you don't trust me to keep my word?"

"I don't think you'd do it on purpose, but..." He pursed his lips. "But sometimes you can be impulsive," he finished.

I snorted. "Okay. Yeah. Sure. I'll give you that." I gave myself a refill and considered what he was saying.

I guess I could get a little impulsive. I didn't really like planning for the future or thinking ahead. And putting my foot in my mouth had bitten me in the ass more than once.

I shifted side-to-side, fidgeting while I thought.

I didn't want to rush Sloane. I didn't want to be overbearing.

Would I be sitting innocently next to her one day, staring into her beautiful eyes, and blurt out she was my mate and I wanted to be with her forever?

That was absolutely something I might do.

She'd think I was too much.

And I'd ruin another relationship. One of the most important relationships I'd ever have.

I ran a hand down my face. "Okay. I'll make a bargain with you."

Bash sighed in relief. "Thank you, Nico."

I put my hand out. "I promise not to tell Sloane about the mating bond."

"And you won't imply what she is to you at all," he amended.

I left my hand hovering in the air. "Yes. I promise not to imply what she is to me at all."

"Agreed." He clasped my hand, and the magic of shadows and flames intertwined up both our arms and sealed the bargain.

He handed me a set of fae cuffs. "So neither of your powers increase more than they already have from being in proximity to one another."

I slipped the cuffs on and asked, "So what exactly is the plan?"

"What do you mean? As soon as Sloane has recovered, the girls will be on the first flight to Delnee."

He took three long strides to the door and disappeared.

"Hold up!" I said, trailing after him. I grabbed his shoulder, but he shrugged me off and went into Sloane's room. Probably because he thought that going into Sloane's room would mean he could avoid the fight we were about to have, but he was wrong.

"That cannot be the plan!" I said.

He yanked me by the arm into the corner of the bedroom, casting nervous eyes at Sloane and Gwen, who were awake and whispering on the bed.

"You're going to send them away? Without telling them anything?" I kept my voice down but just barely.

"Yes," Bash hissed.

Anger ignited inside me. If he didn't want to tell Amaya, that was his own stupid-ass decision to make, but he couldn't make decisions about my relationship with Sloane.

Not that I *had* a relationship with Sloane.

But I'd never *get* one if she was in Delnee while I was here. I couldn't go there either since the Delnee government revoked my travel permit.

And with this Goddess-forsaken bargain, I couldn't even tell her.

"You tricked me." The threat of flames tickled my palms, but the fae cuffs kept my power in check. My dragon roared inside of me. "You can't do this, Bash. She's my—" I gasped and choked, unable to get the word out.

He grimaced. "I'm sorry, Nico." The bedroom door opened. His eyes snapped to Amaya, tracking her as she walked to Sloane's side.

"You can't do this to me. I'm your best friend. This isn't just about you. You can't..." I was angry, but under that anger was an overwhelming sense of betrayal.

Bash knew me better than anyone. He knew that I would make a bargain without asking for more specifics. Without being skeptical. I'd follow my whims in the moment instead of being careful.

He ripped his eyes from Amaya. I was well acquainted with the sight of guilt twisting him up, and I hated being the cause of it, but this was *wrong*.

I crossed my arms and glared at him.

He pressed his lips together. "Fine. I'll negate the bargain with you before they leave, okay? But I can't risk it until then. I can't risk…"

"You can't risk Amaya finding out the truth and actually making a decision for herself?" I hissed.

He frowned. "I can't put her at risk. There is no decision to make. My shadow will hurt or kill her. We can't be together. That's it."

Amaya interrupted our fight—which was probably a good thing—and asked a question about combining their powers to filter the suppression from Sloane's body.

Bash walked over to her.

As mad at him as I was for tricking me into this bargain, I couldn't stay mad for long because he held Amaya's hand to lend her his powers, risking Shadow Bash taking control, in order to clear that awful drug from Sloane's system.

After they were done, her skin seemed less pale, and her eyes became clearer.

I crossed the room and sat in the chair next to the bed.

Determined to play nonchalant, I propped my feet up and said, "Well, Sloane, I hope you like movies, because I'm not letting you leave until you're one hundred and ten percent better."

To distract myself from what I really wanted to do—sit and stare at Sloane for the next six hours straight—I scrolled through our movie options.

"Okay," she said, her response tinny. I watched in my peripheral as she hunkered down in bed.

It was impossible to focus on the movie with my mate right beside me, but I willed my eyes to remain on the screen. The only consolation was that being close to her calmed my dragon and eased the ache in my heart.

<h1 style="text-align:center">Chapter Seven: The Flirt</h1>

Tandem Read to Descend into the Void Chapter 10
Sloane

The superfae movie wasn't keeping my attention. My eyes kept wandering to the male reclined in the chair beside me.

His feet were propped up on the bed, arms crossed over his chest. And *wow*, those arms. Thick and delicious biceps that stretched the sleeves of his shirt. The fabric pulled taut over his sturdy chest.

His auburn hair was loose and wavy, skimming the tops of his shoulders. It looked so soft. I bet it'd fall between my fingertips if I brushed my hands through it.

Lost in a fantasy about touching his hair, I startled when his eyes snapped to mine. My cheeks heated from getting caught staring.

He smiled. It wasn't a cocky, I-know-I'm-attractive smile, more a sweet, you-make-me-happy smile.

I had to look away because that didn't make sense. He didn't know me. There would be no reason I'd make him happy. Something sharp panged in my chest below my collarbone. I rubbed at the spot over my heart to relieve the ache.

He was probably just being polite because I was a traumatized kidnap victim.

The sound of tire squealing on the TV made me flinch. My breathing became erratic; my body tensed, preparing to be tossed into the back of the van, to be burned and healed, burned and healed, stuck in an endless loop of pain. My heartbeat picked up, and adrenaline tried to activate my powers, to push my magic through my veins, but I fought the reaction.

I squeezed my eyes shut, trying to even out my breathing so Gwen and Amaya wouldn't feel the shift in my emotions. I didn't want to talk about it. I didn't want to think about it. I wanted...a distraction. Something. Anything to get me out of the spiral.

A hand landed on my clenched fist. His eyes met mine and flicked toward the remote, a question in his gaze: did I want it turned off?

I gave him a minute shake of my head. The silence would be worse.

His hand left mine, and I felt the loss like a kick to my stomach, but he placed his open palm on the bed in invitation.

We locked gazes. A soupy warm coziness swept through me. His hazel eyes traced my face, something like longing in them, but that couldn't be right.

I'd taken too long to react, and his hand began to retreat, but I snatched it back before he slipped away. I squeezed, clinging to him like his hand was my only lifeline.

Maybe it was.

He cradled my hand, his skin overly warm. A soliser, then. That must have been why I hallucinated him as a dragon. My fantasies of being a heroine in some grand romance had cast the male saving me as the hero in my story.

But didn't the hero usually slay the dragon?

My drug-addled brain must have gotten that part mixed up. I turned the thing I'd feared—the fire, the flames, the heat—into the thing that would save me.

He'd probably laugh if I told him that I imagined him as a dragon. As a high priestess, I had an intuitive sense about people. This male seemed like an easygoing person. His presence reminded me of a concept they taught in high priestess training: if you're falling, you need to resist the urge to clench your body and brace yourself because that was how you broke bones. You had to be loose, to tuck and roll, and allow the impact to move through you, instead of resisting it.

This male embodied that lesson. He rolled with the things most people railed against.

Later on, after he left to make us breakfast, he was a topic that made me feel like I could slip back into myself when Amaya and Gwen were looking at me with concern and pity.

"That is one fine specimen of a male," I'd joked and pretended to fan myself. "They make them different here in Palagui, don't they?"

Especially him. The soliser. My dragon.

I shook my head at that thought. What a silly thing to hallucinate.

Except I wasn't quite so sure it was silly when he came back and Amaya asked him, "Hey, Nico. You know when you told Gwen and I you were a purple-hearted dragon with the biggest cock we'd ever see?"

My sip of water went down the wrong pipe, and I coughed.

Was he actually a dragon?

And why was that not the part of the sentence my mind was most stuck on?

I could hear the smugness in his grin as he said, "Yeah."

"How did you trick Gwen's power into not knowing you were lying?" Amaya asked.

I kept my eyes on my plate as he explained that he could trick empaths' powers by weaving truth into a lie. He'd focus on the part of the sentence that was true so his feelings would align.

I didn't meet his eye as we finished our breakfast, and instead, tried to figure out which part of his statement was the truth.

***

Amaya and Gwen were out of control.

I couldn't make even the slightest movement without both of their eyes darting to me. If I reached over to the nightstand for my glass of water, one of them would jump up to get it. They brought all my food to me in bed. They even insisted on waiting in the bathroom when I showered, in case I became weak.

It might have been a reasonable worry at first, but I hadn't had a dizzy spell since the first day.

My physical strength was back. I was *fine*.

Mostly fine.

I mean, maybe not mentally fine, but I certainly wasn't at risk of falling in the shower.

I knew they were worried. I knew they were only trying to help.

But I didn't know how much more of this I could take.

They took shifts in their job of *watching Sloane's every move*. If one of them left to nap or shower, the other was always right there.

I didn't have a single moment to myself.

Nico was the only one who didn't treat me like a broken baby bird.

He didn't ask if I needed help. He didn't ask if I wanted to talk. He didn't tell me he was here for me.

He didn't have to.

He was always just there, watching movies with me or telling me jokes. His easy, steady presence said it all. An offer of support without the accompanying pity or concern.

Sometimes the car noises in the movies we watched made me flinch, or I'd space out, staring at the walls, reliving the feeling of burning alive and not being able to escape.

Gwen or Amaya would shake me out of it, and I'd force myself to push away those feelings so they couldn't sense them.

But Nico never reacted. He'd leave his hand, palm up, on the bedspread near my thigh.

An invitation for comfort, but no pressure.

His open hand said that he was there for me if I wanted to reach out. I didn't have to manage my emotions to alleviate his.

My best friends were wonderful, and I loved them. I didn't blame them for being overprotective, but Nico was the only person I didn't have to try to be okay for. I could be whoever I was in that moment. Lost in a flashback, sad, or…on some occasions, I could distract myself by slipping back into the girl I used to be.

"I'm going to shower," I said, flinging off the bed covers. "Alone," I added when Gwen started to stand.

"Are you sure…?"

"Yes, Gwen. I'm capable of washing myself without any help." I couldn't keep the annoyance from my voice this time.

"You sure about that?" Nico said with a taunting smirk.

I narrowed my eyes at him, fighting a smile. "Yes."

He ran his tongue over his bottom lip and shrugged one shoulder. "I'd be more than happy to assist you if you needed it."

I could feel my body sliding into my old self, like the perfect pair of jeans. My hip jutted out, eyes squinting into a flirty expression.

I opened my mouth to give him some witty retort, but Gwen cut me off with a sharp inhaled breath. "What the hell?" she said. "You aren't going to touch her!"

My eyes widened in her direction. "It was obviously a joke."

"It wasn't though," she said with a huff. "I know if I left this room, he'd try something on you."

She rounded the bed, her hands on her hips, trying to tower over Nico, but even sitting down, he was bigger than her.

"It really was just a joke," Nico said. He put his hands out like he was showing he had no ulterior motives. "Sloane looked like she needed a laugh."

He looked at me over Gwen's shoulder, and I bit my lip, smiling softly.

"Your jokes aren't funny," Gwen said. "Don't think I forgot that you tried to hit on me the second I walked in the door. You probably did the same to Amaya too. I know your game, fire breather."

"I'm sorry. Won't happen again, okay?" Nico stared at Gwen with wide-eyed sincerity. "I'm not going to try anything."

My stomach sank. I wanted him to try something. I wanted his flirting. I wanted his jokes.

"Gwen…" I put my hand on her shoulder. "Let up, okay? I'm going to shower. And maybe you should too? I know you're trying to protect me, but I need a little space to breathe."

She exhaled a long sigh, but then finally said, "Okay. If you're sure."

She turned, and I pulled her into a hug so she'd stop glaring at Nico. "I'm sure."

I looked at Nico over Gwen's shoulder as I rubbed her back. There was a little worried crease between his eyebrows. It was the first time his larger-than-life presence seemed small.

I winked at him as reassurance.

A wide grin broke out over his face, all of his perfect white teeth showing. My heart hurt looking at him.

He pushed himself up out of the chair and left the room, and Gwen followed behind him.

I had twenty blissful minutes of solitude.

When my fingers started pruning, I grudgingly got out of the shower and wrapped a towel around my body.

As I opened the door to go back into the bedroom, there was a gasp.

"Sorry!" Nico said. "Sorry. I swear—" He slapped a hand over his eyes. "I swear I wasn't trying to be a creep." He held up his phone with one hand. "I forgot this on the chair. I wasn't like waiting for you or going to do anything—"

"Nico."

"In fact, if you want me to leave you alone for good—"

"Nico."

"—I'll stay away, no questions asked. I just have terrible timing—"

"Nico!"

"Yeah?"

"Will you please put your hand down? I'm in a towel, not stark naked."

He spread his fingers, peeking out, and then snapped them closed. "I better not."

I giggled.

He smiled. "Don't want you to think I came in here for any nefarious reasons."

I shook my head, even though he couldn't see it. "Okay, fine. If I go put some clothes on, will you promise to be here when I come out?"

He rubbed the back of his neck with the hand that wasn't covering his eyes and started shifting left and right. "If Gwen…"

I walked over to the bedroom door and turned the lock with an audible click.

When I turned back, I watched his throat work in a hard swallow.

"Yeah…" he said. "I'll, ah…" He put his hand out, feeling through the air for the chair since his eyes were squeezed shut. "I'll wait here."

I chuckled, grabbed my clothes, and put them on in the bathroom as fast as possible.

Nico's hazel eyes darted to me when I walked out, though they seemed to get snagged on my legs, which were on display in my shorts.

He refocused his gaze on the ground as I arranged myself on the bed near his chair, my knees almost brushing his.

"Seriously, sorry about this." Wincing, he held up his phone. "I'm pretty forgetful."

I grabbed his hand and patted it. "Don't take anything Gwen's says seriously. She's just protective. You didn't do anything wrong."

His chest inflated with breath. "She can be a little intense."

My hand, without my conscious permission, shifted from patting his hand to caressing his arm with the backs of my fingers. "She's my best friend. That's how she shows that she cares…" I shrugged.

Nico shifted, and our legs touched. We both leaned in, closing the distance between our faces. Most of his auburn hair was pulled back at the nape of his neck, but a single piece was loose and curled near his chin.

"And is that how you want to be cared for?" he asked.

I furrowed my brow. I'd never considered that I might have a preference for how I'd want my friend to treat me. "I…I don't know. This is just how we are together. I guess it can sometimes get to be a bit…too much."

Nico's smile didn't fall exactly, but it seemed to lose its vibrance. "Right. Too much. So you're not a fan of too much."

"Is anyone?" I joked.

He huffed a weird laugh and looked away. "No. I guess not."

Nico had a strong profile, high forehead and big nose, a cut jaw covered by an auburn beard. He reminded me of fur pelts and cold winter nights. This close, his sweet, smoky musk filled my head with images of sweaty naked bodies writhing on a thick cozy rug in front of a fireplace. Specifically, his naked body and my naked body.

Oh my.

I leaned back a little to gather my wits and shake myself free of those images. "So I just wanted to tell you…" I started and stopped, getting flustered by his nearness. "I, uh, wanted to say you can joke with me. I don't mind."

He pinned me with his smoldering gaze. The corner of his mouth quirked up. "If I'm being honest, it was more like flirting than joking really…"

I bit my bottom lip. "I noticed."

"It doesn't make you uncomfortable?"

I shook my head. My eyes hooded as our faces were drawn closer to one another, lips only inches apart. "I like it," I whispered, my voice ragged and husky.

"Do you?" His gaze locked on my mouth.

The sound of the doorknob jiggling broke us apart.

"Sloane?" Amaya called out.

I sighed. Nico jumped up, turning to search the chair for his phone.

"I should go," he said, pocketing his device and darting toward the door. He unlocked it and breezed by Amaya.

She stood at the threshold, stunned, and blinked a few times before saying, "What did I interrupt there?"

"Nothing," I said, but my heart's rapid fluttering didn't agree with that answer.

"Uh huh. Sure," Amaya said in a suspicious sing-song voice, clearly not buying it either.

Chapter Eight: The Itch

Nico

"I just…" Bash's sigh teleported his weariness through the phone. "I can't be around her. What if something happens again and my power grows? I can't control my shadow as it is."

"Alright," I said. "But what am I supposed to tell them? You've been gone for weeks."

I hated that he was putting me in this position. It didn't take an empath to know Amaya was upset that he'd disappeared after he made out with her in his bedroom.

"Tell them I'm handling business in Merbany," Bash said. "It's not like they're going to know that's out of the ordinary."

"Alright."

"I'm sorry, Nico."

We hung up, and it was my turn to sigh.

I'd just gotten home from boxing at the gym downtown. I'd been needing to bloody up my knuckles more than usual lately. There was this constant ache in my chest; it gnawed at me and made my dragon antsy and restless.

I wanted to fly. The urge to shift prickled under my skin. My power was hungry for something I couldn't give it.

Sloane was still recovering. She had good and bad days.

Sometimes we'd spend the whole evening goofing off together. Her green eyes glistened with flecks of gold when she was joking with me. Her vibrance was the most beautiful thing I'd ever witnessed.

But some days her light was dimmed, and when my attempts to coax her out of a memory didn't work, I didn't force it. On those quiet days, I did my best to bank the fire, giving her space and a hand to hold. You couldn't force a spark to catch. You could only give it the tinder it needed to blaze.

It took me far too long to figure out car noises were her trigger, but then her refusal to leave the house made sense. I stopped suggesting we watch action movies and called my fae healing therapist, Karina, to put down a deposit for a session.

Karina had a long waiting list, so if Sloane didn't need or want the appointment when the time came around, there was always someone at the veteran's office I could give the spot to. It'd taken me a long time after coming home from the war to admit I was struggling, and even longer to get help, but the guys at the office had been a lifeline when I was drowning.

I hoped I could be that for Sloane.

Slipping on my gold fae cuffs—the ones that had been passed down in my family for generations—I walked down the hall to Sloane's room and knocked on her door.

"Come in," Sloane said.

As I walked in, dueling emotions warred in my heart. Pleasure from seeing her and pain that I couldn't kiss her.

"I knew it was you," she said.

I made my way to the chair near the bed. It was just the two of us for now. Gwen said last night she was having dinner with Caroline, and Amaya had been giving Sloane more alone time lately.

"How did you know it was me?" I asked.

She patted the space beside her on the bed and scooted over. I took her offer, and she snuggled in close. She'd been inviting me onto the bed with her ever since I mentioned that I'd been a prisoner of war. I hadn't needed the comfort—I'd long ago worked through the worst of those memories, but no way in hell was I going to turn down her cuddles.

"It's weird. It's like I had this feeling." She waved a hand over her chest.

"That's not weird. It's actually really common for m—" I coughed as my throat closed up, and my body broke out into invisible hives.

Shit.

I scratched my arms and tried to focus on thinking about anything other than mates and mating bonds and Sloane.

Which was impossible sitting right next to her.

She handed me a glass of water when I kept coughing and patted my back until my fit died down.

"Common for?" Sloane prompted.

I scratched my legs. "Uh..."

Instead of pushing me to answer, she climbed out of bed and went into the bathroom.

My arms and legs and torso were prickling like fire ants were biting me. I wanted to jump out of my skin.

I laid back and closed my eyes, trying to stop scratching.

I'd been tortured for years, but I can say with utmost certainty that being itchy is worse than any pain I'd ever endured.

I could dissociate from pain.

Itching?

There was no escape.

I squinted my eyes open when Sloane came out of the bathroom. She walked to the side of the bed and flipped off the top of a lotion bottle.

"I asked Gwen to get this," she said. "Told her I had some scars I wanted to get rid of."

I growled. "You do? They scarred you?"

She put her hand on my shoulder and pushed me back down with more force than I'd have thought someone her size would have. "No. I fibbed a little because I wanted her to buy me this. It has a calming extract. I thought..." She worried her lip and looked at the arm I was tearing apart with my fingernails.

Determination filled her eyes, and she squeezed lotion into her hand.

I blamed the itching for distracting me. I didn't realize what she was going to do until the cold cream was on my arm and she was massaging it into my skin.

My eyes closed, and I barely held back a moan. Her hands on me. Even just my arm. Goddess, it was the most erotic thing I'd ever felt.

"It's odd," she said. "Your skin looks healthy. There are no patches or dry skin. Only the scratch marks..."

"Psychosomatic," I hissed through my teeth. Karina taught me that word. The body produced feelings that had no physical cause. Like the phantom pains of my old war wounds. The bargain induced a mental trance that caused intense itching. If I continued to push the bargain, my body would likely produce actual hives and who knows what else as a stress response.

She hummed and squeezed more lotion into her hands, leaning over my body to reach the other arm. I screwed my eyes closed so I didn't focus on her chest pressing into mine.

The itching was stopping. But only because now I was trying to will my boner away.

"I..." She cleared her throat. "I could get your back...if you wanted."

I blinked up at her and looked between her eyes. Was she actually just helping me or did she want to touch me?

"Wow. I'm sorry," she said. Her cheeks flushed. "I'm usually a lot better at flirting than this. I..." She grimaced. "You make me really nervous."

I sat up, concerned. Though other parts of my body wanted to focus on the flirting aspect of her comment.

"I make you nervous?" I asked, shaking my head. "I don't want you to be nervous around me. Did I do something to make you feel that way? Or tell me what I can do to make you more comfortable."

The corner of her mouth quirked up, and heat filled her eyes. "You could take off your shirt. I think that'd make me more comfortable," she whispered.

Surprise delayed my movements, my brain short-circuiting, but then I reacted in a flash, reaching one arm back and yanking off my shirt.

She giggled and crawled onto the bed, kneeling behind me. The cap of the lotion popped off again.

I jolted as the cold cream touched my upper back, but it wasn't from the temperature. This time I couldn't stop my low moan from escaping as she dug her fingers into the muscles of my shoulders. After my workout, her hands felt like heaven, loosening and relaxing every part of me.

Well, every part of me except the one that was very hard now.

"That feels really good, Sloane."

"Mmm," she said. Her breath at the back of my ear made me shiver. "You're so big." Her thumbs massaged down the muscles on either side of my spine and swooped up to the front, pressing into my pecs. "So strong."

"Goddess, female. You really are good at this flirting thing. Stroke my ego some more."

"Or I could stroke something else," she said, and her teeth nipped at my ear. Her fingers traced the outline of the soliser sun tattoo on my sternum.

My eyes widened, and my cock strained against the zipper of my jeans. "Sloane," I said and turned around.

She raised her eyebrows in question. Her green eyes glinted with mischief.

Goddess she was beautiful. So fucking beautiful.

"I don't..." I swallowed. I wanted to flirt with her. I wanted to do so much more than flirt with her, but I didn't know what was going on. This was far more than the friendly teasing banter that we usually had.

She deflated; despair filled her eyes as she ran a finger across my shoulder. "I just want to be normal again, Nico."

Ah.

She'd planned this. The lotion? The massage?

She wanted to be the girl who didn't stare off into space or jump at the sound of car doors slamming.

If flirting with me made her feel normal, I'd get on board. I could volley it back.

I grabbed her hand and pulled so she had to lean over and catch herself. Smiling as her face came within inches of mine, I said, "You can stroke any part of me, any time you want."

Her tongue darted out and licked her bottom lip. "Such a dirty mind. What would Gwen say?"

I snorted. "Gwen wouldn't have let me take off my shirt."

"True. It'd probably burn her eyes." She ran a hand over my chest and up both sides of my neck. "All this hotness."

I groaned good-naturedly. "Are these soliser jokes?"

She laughed. "Maybe. It's just too easy."

I snatched the lotion from her hand. "My turn for stroking. Lie down."

Her eyes got wide, but she scurried to get situated. We rearranged so she was lying down and I was near her feet. Her chest moved up and down in heavy pants as she watched me.

I momentarily forgot what I was doing, watching her cleavage spilling from the top of her shirt. Practically begging for my mouth.

"Where are you going to stroke me, Nico?" She tossed her hands over her head, and the seductive line her body made was making me stupid. The curve of her breasts, the nip of her waist, the swell of her thighs, the little wiggle of her hips.

I was salivating. I wanted my mouth all over her.

"You're playing with fire, baby," I said.

She giggled.

I blinked and shook myself out of my trance. "I only meant your feet." I grabbed her ankle and put her foot on my lap.

She crossed her hands under her head and flicked her toes. "That'll do for now," she said haughtily.

I put lotion on my hands and dug my thumbs into her foot, watching her face as I pressed into the arch. Her eyes rolled back, and her body went limp.

Did I think touching her feet would be the safest place?

Because I was wrong.

She was breathing hard and making little noises of pleasure when I found a knot.

There was no hiding my erection, especially when her other foot moved on my lap and stroked over my hard length.

I inhaled sharply.

She smirked and opened an eye. "Oops."

I huffed a breath. "Oops?"

She gave a little shrug. "My bad."

This girl was going to kill me.

As I switched to the other foot, she let her leg fall open.

My nostrils flared. The scent of her arousal drifted through the room, unconcealed by the thin cotton shorts she was wearing. My eyes snapped to the space between her parted legs. Her red panties peeked out.

She was wet for me. And she wanted me to know it.

All that separated my gaze from her glistening pussy was little pieces of fabric.

I swallowed.

Goddess, I wanted her so damn bad.

But this was just a distraction for her, a way to feel normal. I couldn't tell her I wanted more. With this damn bargain, I couldn't tell her how I felt at all.

I put her foot down and stood from the bed.

This wouldn't last forever. Soon enough, I'd tell her. Bash would let me out of this bargain and then I could form the word *mate*.

Just thinking it made my arms itch.

"I…uh…Do you…Do you want to play a game?"

"What kind of game?"

"A card game."

Her grin was wicked. "Like strip poker?"

"No." I closed my eyes and ran a hand down my face, trying not to picture her stripping for me. "No. No. No stripping. Clothes. Stay. On." To prove my point, I bent down and pulled on my shirt.

She pouted, and I opened the nightstand drawer to pull out a pack of cards.

Her flirty eyes fell away, and a faint tinge of red bloomed on her cheeks. She crossed her legs and sat up on the bed with a rigid posture. "Oh yeah. Sure."

I sighed in relief because I'm pretty sure if she said "No, I'd like you to fuck me," I wouldn't have had the strength to deny her.

We sat as far away from one another as I could manage to get while still being able to play the game.

She wouldn't meet my eye the rest of the night. I didn't know how to tell her she didn't have to be embarrassed without explaining why I clammed up.

So instead, I ignored it, and focused on teaching her a card game while thinking entirely innocent thoughts.

Chapter Nine: The Light

Sloane

Nico did not sit still.

There was always a part of him in motion. His knee jiggled. He twirled pens between his fingers. He paced. He fidgeted. His body ping-ponged around the room as much as the topics of our conversations did.

He was a never-ending ball of energy.

And he was a never-ending source of light. He always had a smile for me. A joke. A story about his kids that he trained at the high school.

He was my favorite part of the day. An effervescent joy bubbled inside me when he was around, making me forget about the numb, hollow spaces that had been carved in my heart.

"Sorry for being late," he said in a rush, closing my bedroom door behind him. His auburn hair was loose and wild around his shoulders.

"It's okay. Did something happen?"

"Nothing bad. I didn't mean to worry you, but I don't have your number, so I couldn't text you," he said and flopped on to the bed hard enough that I bounced a little from the other side.

I giggled. "Is that your sly way of asking for my number?"

His mouth opened and then closed, eyebrows pulling together. "Actually, no. I'm not exactly known for being sly."

I snorted.

He smirked and crawled over to my side of the bed. "Hey pretty lady, can I get your number?"

I pretended to think about it by tapping a finger on my chin. "Well, okay, but only since you asked so directly."

He tossed his phone onto my lap, and I put my number in his contacts.

"So did you just get held up? Or were those same two boys fighting after school again? What were their names? Rollin and George?" I asked.

"Yeah, but no, it wasn't them this time," he said, lounging back on the bed, remote in his hand. "Someone accidentally slashed my tires."

"What?" I screeched, dropping the phone.

He shrugged. "Had to call for a tow."

"Wait, accidentally?"

He nodded.

"How do you know it was an accident?"

He launched up and walked to the end of the bed, needing lots of space to move when he was regaling me with a story. Practically, acting it out.

He put his hands up. "So I came out of school, walked to my car, and BAM!"—he smacked his hands together—"I see that two of my tires are flat. And I was thinking to myself, *What the hell. I don't have any enemies. Who would ever do this to me?*"

I was fighting my laughter and nodded along.

"I cross the parking lot and make it to the driver side door, right? Then, POP!"—his fingers spread out like an explosion—"A head springs up near the tire on the passenger side. A female dressed in all black, like something straight out of a movie. Her eyes got real wide, and she says, *Is this your car?*"

I put my hand over my mouth and shouted, "No way!"

He bobbed his head vigorously with a big grin. "And I said to her, *Yeah, it is. Why are you slashing my tires?*"

Holding his stomach as he laughed, he managed to get out, "And she says, *My ex-boyfriend has the same car. I thought this was it.*"

My jaw dropped. "Oh my Goddess."

"So I asked, *Who's your ex?* And she told me his name. Turns out it was this asshole guy who works in the administration office. I looked around the parking lot and pointed to his car. I knew it was his because this dick had a Solisers Are Light Bringers bumper sticker."

"Wait. You didn't yell at her for slashing your tires?"

Nico shook his head, aghast. "Hell no. Poor girl was in a relationship with a factionist asshole. I would have helped her slash his tires if she asked. She ran to his car, got the job done, and apologized for the mix-up. Gave me a ride home after I called the tow truck. Nice girl. The ex-boyfriend drained her bank account, so she couldn't offer to pay for new tires, but she works at a restaurant downtown and gave me a gift card for the place so..." He shrugged, smiling.

I just shook my head at him. Anyone else would have been livid, but nothing bothered Nico. He was happy and free and...perfect.

"You're incredible," I said.

He glanced at me with a confused smile. "Thanks?"

I wanted to grab his face and kiss him.

Having finished his story, he climbed back into bed. "So do you want to use the gift card with me?"

My face fell. I opened my mouth, but no words came out.

He shrugged off my nonresponse and focused on the TV. "No big deal. Just an idea."

"Nico..."

He waved a dismissive hand. "No worries, Sloane."

But I didn't want to leave things this way. "It's not you. It's me."

He cringed and cast his eyes away, but I brought my hand to his jaw and turned his face back. My fingers stroked his soft auburn facial hair.

"No. Seriously," I said. "If I was ready to leave the house, I'd want to go with you."

He covered my hand with his and interlaced our fingers. "Then there's no expiration on the offer."

Our hands fell, but remained intertwined. I dropped his gaze, staring at how his big palm engulfed mine completely, protectively.

In a tiny voice, I said, "Okay."

Chapter Ten: The Flashback

Sloane

My bedroom was dark except for the light from the TV flickering on the walls. I didn't remember falling asleep. My legs were tangled in a blanket, and my head was resting on a very warm, very cuddly pillow.

Nope. Not a pillow.

I peeked up from my position on his chest, and our eyes met.

Shadows and light danced on his face from the TV. Murmurs from the movie we were watching filled the room, but they didn't penetrate the little bubble encasing us. I waited for him to pull away, but he only shifted us so we were both on our sides, face-to-face.

"I fell asleep," he said, his voice sexy and gravelly.

"It's okay."

Neither of us said anything else, just stared at each other, breathing each other's air. His hand was on my hip, in a perfectly chaste place, but still, desire pooled low in my stomach.

He looked so kissable, his lips soft and plump. I wanted to know if he'd taste how he smelled. Sweet and smoky. I wanted to know what it felt like to have my body under his, to be entirely covered by him. He was big enough that I could disappear if he wrapped his arms around me.

He inched closer with a steady focus on my mouth. Whatever protests he had against taking our relationship further must have dissolved in the sleepy limbo we'd awakened into.

"Sloane," he whispered, heavy with longing. I closed my eyes and waited for the press of his lips—

Screech.

My body locked up as the harsh noise on the TV pierced through the soft veil of comfort Nico had covered me in.

Fear broke out as a cold sweat. I couldn't move, couldn't speak, couldn't think. I squeezed my eyes closed and waited for the moment the flames would lick my skin, unable to do anything to stop the burn. My power tried to flare to life, but I forced it down. If I healed myself, the burns would continue longer. I couldn't use my power. I could only hope for the relief of passing out to escape the agony.

A hand grabbed my arm, and I choked back a sob. The hand disappeared.

"Sloane." Someone was saying my name. Repeating it.

Tears leaked from the corners of my eyes. I panted, chest heaving, trying to suck in air, my last bit of breath before the smoke and flames would suffocate me.

"It's okay, Sloane. You're in Palagui. You're in the townhouse. You're in bed with me, and there's a blanket on your left leg. Can you feel it? Can you feel the pillow under your head?"

I whimpered, but something about his voice overrode the fear, like he could speak directly to my soul.

Awareness of a fleece blanket on my foot trickled in.

"I can smell the strawberry of your shampoo," he said. "And the eucalyptus from the lotion you put on my arms earlier. Can you smell that?"

Somehow, I was able to inhale. I focused on the scents he was describing. There was the eucalyptus, and even more potent than that, was his sweet smokiness.

My shoulders fell as tension bled out of me.

Nico. Nico. Nico. His name was my mantra. I reached out to grab on to him. Hard muscle covered with a thick, cuddly layer of flab. I pressed my nose into the place on his body with the strongest scent and breathed him in, let his essence fill me, surround me.

His hand was on me again, but I didn't flinch this time. He held me. His fingers spread across my back, between my shoulder blades, pressing me to him, anchoring me.

I dragged my nose from his armpit, along his chest, and to his neck. Something instinctual in me had my teeth aching, and without thought, I bit down on the skin of his neck.

Oh. His skin tasted so good.

Like a deranged person, I started licking and sucking his neck. His sweet smoky scent translated into a delicious taste on my tongue. He moaned my name, and I jolted back, my hand covering my mouth.

"Oh Goddess. I'm so sorry. I don't know why I did that." I scrambled to the other side of the bed.

"It's okay, Sloane. It's fine. You were having a flashback," he said.

He sat up. One side of his hair was wild and frizzy, and his shirt was rumpled.

Even in the dark, the sweet concern in his hazel eyes was shining bright. It made my heart ache.

He was...Goddess. He was so gorgeous.

Not just my heart, but every part of me ached for him. The place between my thighs throbbed, needy and ready for his touch, despite having a trauma response a few seconds ago. Maybe *because* I was scared. Maybe my body knew he'd protect me, wrap me up in the safety of his presence like he had in the research center.

Oh boy. I wanted him so bad.

I'd never wanted anyone so bad in my entire life. My power maturity wasn't even this intense.

"I'm really sorry," I breathed out.

"It's okay." He grabbed the remote and muted the TV.

"I didn't mean to, uh, lick you."

The corner of his mouth quirked up. "It's okay."

I averted my gaze so I didn't do something crazy like asking if I could do it again.

He chuckled a little. "We could even the score if that'll make you feel better. Do you want me to lick you?"

My eyes widened as they swung to him.

Cringing, he ran a hand down his face. "That didn't come out right."

I huffed out a little laugh, and he grinned.

Then intense, side-splitting laughter overtook us both. I couldn't stop. Tears formed in my eyes as I gasped for breath. A soul-clearing catharsis. Like Nico was helping me move through my nervous system's fight-or-flight response with stomach-cramping laughter.

"I always say things without thinking about what I'm actually saying," he said when we finally caught our breath.

"It's okay," I said, wiping my eyes. "I like that you always make me laugh, Nico."

His lips spread across his face in the widest grin, like I'd given him the best gift in the world.

I knee-walked back to his side of the bed. Sitting beside him, I stared at my hands as the heat of shame filled my cheeks, and I whispered, "Thank you for bringing me out of it."

"I used to get flashbacks all the time, Sloane. It's nothing to be embarrassed about."

"From the war?"

He nodded.

I used a finger to trace little shapes on the top of his hand. "How long were you…?"

"I was in the military for sixty years, then got captured and held for about twenty." He took a deep breath. "It's weird to think about honestly. That I have been free for as long as I had been imprisoned."

I clenched my fists. My power tried to flicker alive from the heat of anger and helplessness churning in my core, but I shoved it down. "That's terrible. I'm so sorry you went through that. Just thinking about"—my voice cracked—"about someone hurting you, it makes me want to do terrible violent things, and I'm really not a violent person."

"I know, Sloane," he said, soft. "It's okay. I'm okay. I don't get flashbacks anymore. Those memories don't haunt me like they used to. I focus on living my life in the present as much as possible."

I looked into his hazel eyes and saw the truth of him. Nico's boundless energy might have been a trait that he was born with, but he had to learn to choose joy, to harness that energy into a positive perspective, even though anger and grief were perfectly understandable emotional reactions to what he'd been through.

I swallowed. "How did you stop having flashbacks?"

He interlaced his fingers with mine. "I got help. It was hard for a while, and then it got better."

I didn't have a response to that.

After we sat in silence for a few minutes, he asked, "Do you want help, Sloane?"

I worried my lip. Part of me believed that Nico was just strong, certainly stronger than me. I didn't think there was anything anyone could do. My mind associated my healing magic with the pain that came from being burned.

I wanted to get better. I wanted to leave the house and watch movies without jumping from car noises.

I just didn't know if I could, and disappointing him—disappointing myself—would be worse than learning to live without my power.

"Maybe," I hedged.

He squeezed my hand. "Okay. You tell me when you're ready."

I nodded as my tears fell onto our hands.

He cupped my jaw, and his thumbs wiped under my eyes.

He didn't tell me not to cry. He didn't tell me it would be okay.

He was just there.

"I should probably go," he said.

"Stay."

He pressed his lips into a thin line. Indecision flickered in his eyes, some internal battle I didn't understand.

"Please? I don't want to be alone," I said.

He exhaled a breath and wrapped his arms around me, hugging me. I buried my face into his chest and tucked in closer.

"I'll always be here for you, Sloane. Whenever you need me."

"Thank you."

We stayed like that for a while, until my eyes got heavy. Nico reached for the remote and turned off the TV, and we hunkered down into the covers.

But before I could curl up next to him, he cleared his throat. Tilting his head, he motioned to his lower body. "Would you mind if I, uh, took my sweatpants off? I get really hot at night."

"Sure. Of course."

He reached under the covers and pulled them off, chucking them on the floor next to the bed.

"You can take off your shirt too," I said, barely stopping myself before adding *please*.

"You sure it won't make you uncomfortable?"

"Nope." *Not in the way you're implying.*

He pulled off his shirt, and discarded it with the sweatpants.

After he was situated, I pressed my face into his arm and hiked my leg over his hips. My body revved up from having so much access to his bare skin. I outlined the sun tattoo on his sternum with my fingertip, tracing the wavy soliser initiation tattoo.

"I want to hold you," he said, adjusting his arm so it was under my head, the other resting on my thigh. "But, uhm, you may notice a certain bodily reaction to the fact that a gorgeous girl is in bed with me. I just don't want you to be alarmed."

I huffed a laugh. If it was anyone else, I would have teased him by wiggling my hips until I found his "bodily reaction."

But it was Nico, and he was skittish about our attraction. I didn't want to do anything that would make him leave, so I said, "Don't worry. I'm not afraid of your boner."

He dipped his chin. "Right. Okay. Very good."

I nuzzled into him, and his heat seeped into me as I rested my head on his chest. "G'night, Nico."

He stroked the top of my arm, lulling me to sleep. "Goodnight, Sloane."

Chapter Eleven: The Move

Sloane

Nico laughed and flung his cards down. "You're doing it wrong!"

"No, I'm not!" I grinned, but yeah, I *was* doing it wrong.

When he first explained this game, it didn't seem that hard, but every time he outlined the rules, I got a little…distracted.

He rolled his eyes good-naturedly as he launched into another overview. "Okay, so if you pull a number less than ten…"

He curled a long, wavy piece of auburn hair behind his ear. Beautiful, earnest hazel eyes locked on mine. Thick auburn facial hair surrounded his plush and kissable mouth. A plush kissable mouth that I'd almost had against mine.

"But if you pull something that adds up to more than…"

He was so gorgeous. His shoulders and biceps and torso were thick with muscle, but it wasn't the hard cut of a body builder. There was a fluffy bulk to him. I had loved feeling his soft round stomach pressed against me while we cuddled last night. His big, hefty arms, holding me, keeping me safe from everything bad in the world.

"And if I have cards that add up to more than ten, but you have cards that are less than…"

I felt that extremely not soft part of him too. I'd woken up to his hard length pressed to my backside. As soon as my body registered it, I was flooded with want. My clit throbbed, and my breasts felt heavy and aching. When he stirred awake, he tried to angle his hips away, but it didn't help much because he was just so...big.

I was starting to think he was definitely not a dragon, and that the true part of his statement to Amaya and Gwen had been—

"Sloane?" A hand waved in front of my eyes.

He crossed his arms, trying to look stern. "Are you listening?

"Uh huh."

"What did I just say?"

"That if your cards add up to ten..." I trailed off.

"Yeah?" he prompted, eyes twinkling.

I narrowed my eyes in concentration. "I win?"

He looked to the ceiling like he was praying to the Goddess for help. "You are unteachable."

I sucked in a breath and put a hand over my heart. "I thought you were the best teacher in all of Palagui?"

He shook his head. "Some people are too far gone, even for me."

I leaned over and shoved his shoulder. "Hey! Maybe you shouldn't give up on your students so quickly."

Laughing, he retaliated by nudging my leg with his. I kicked out my foot and pressed it into his belly.

He grunted and grabbed my ankle, yanking it so I fell back on the bed, and then, he crawled up over my body. "Didn't anyone ever teach you to pick on people your own size?"

His arms were on either side of my torso, and his bent knees brushed the outside of my hips, only a thin sliver of air separating us.

Our smiles faded. The teasing humor in his eyes shifted into molten lust.

"Well, I'm unteachable so..." I whispered with a trembling breath.

His eyes devoured my body, tracing my face, lingering on my lips before sliding down my throat and to my chest. The heat of his gaze was burning through the little restraint I had left.

"Sloane." My name was a plea.

"Kiss me," I said in answer to the question he didn't ask.

His face scrunched up as if he was fumbling for restraint as well. He closed his eyes and exhaled slow.

"Nico." I ran my hands along his muscular forearms and biceps and squeezed the bulky build of his shoulders. "Kiss me, please."

I wasn't sure why he was reluctant to take things between us to the next level. I knew he liked me, and I had evidence of his want pressed against my backside this morning.

He certainly wasn't shy, although he had been very careful to always make sure I was comfortable, so maybe Gwen's threats were part of his resistance.

All I knew for sure was that I wanted him.

Desperately.

More than I'd ever wanted anyone in my entire life.

With a heavy sigh, he leaned back and got off the bed. I sat up in tandem as if my body couldn't stand the thought of being too far from his.

He gathered his hair in both hands and tied it into a low bun. He always put his hair up when he needed to think. I guess if it was loose, his thoughts were too scattered.

"Nico?" My voice was puny. Embarrassment heated my cheeks.

His long strides ate up the room as he paced. "I need to tell you something."

He scratched at his arms, both at the same time. That was another thing he always did. Scratching. So much scratching.

It had to be a nervous tick of sorts. He would always start itching when he was flustered about something. Psychosomatic, he'd explained.

"Okay..." I said.

He scratched at his chest, frantic. With a deep breath, he squeezed his hands into fists, thrust them behind his back, and stopped in front of me. "I've never really been in a relationship before."

I squinted my eyes. "Okay."

"I've dated a lot, but it's never been..." His gaze fell to the floor, and his shoulders hunched forward.

"Been?"

"More. More than regular fuck buddies or a couple months of dating. Never like commitment and long-term plans and expectations."

I furrowed my brows. "I'm not asking for your hand in marriage, Nico. I thought there was some mutual attraction here, but if I'm wrong..." I trailed off, waiting for him to confirm or deny.

His eyebrows turned downward, and he chewed on his lip, not meeting my gaze.

"Oh." The heat in my cheeks traveled to my chest. I'd gotten this wrong. So very wrong.

Nico was a nice guy, the nicest guy. He'd been hanging out with me because I was a traumatized kidnap victim. He stayed with me last night because I asked him to. He flirted with me because I told him I wanted to feel normal. Yeah, he was attracted to me, but he even said that it was a bodily reaction to having a girl next to him in bed.

That didn't mean he liked me.

He was just being nice, and I was seeing things that weren't there.

I started to get up. I didn't know where I was going to go. Crawl in a hole maybe, but he trapped me with his arms on either side of my hips.

"Sloane. No—" He closed his eyes. "You're m—"

Sparks began popping along his arms.

"Nico!"

He jumped up, and his eyes widened in horror as he stared at his arms. They were bright red with hives. The red patches spread up his neck too.

"Oh Goddess!" I ran to the dresser to grab the lotion, but Nico was backing away, shaking his head.

"I'm sorry, Sloane." His eyes were lost, almost hopeless. "I can't...I can't do this with you."

The red hives on his skin were changing. Sparks continued flickering, making his skin almost appear an iridescent golden-orange.

He was out the door and sprinting down the hall before I could get a better look.

His itching had been psychosomatic, but apparently his stress was manifesting as actual symptoms now, reacting with his fire powers.

Me. I was stressing him out. I was giving him hives because I kept throwing myself at him and he was too nice of a guy to say he didn't like me that way.

I pressed the backs of my hands to my hot cheeks, but nothing was going to cool the burn of my embarrassment.

Chapter Twelve: The Fake Out

Tandem Read to Descend into the Void Chapter 11
Sloane

At some point, Nico and I made the unspoken promise to pretend he didn't run away when I asked him to kiss me.

He still hung out in my bedroom after work, but only if Amaya and Gwen were around too.

I'd thought things would be awkward between us, that we'd stop touching and cuddling, but it was like nothing happened at all. He still snuggled up beside me while we all watched movies, his arm behind my head on the pillow, the side of his body pressed to mine.

I spent more time wondering what was going on than paying attention to the movie. He certainly wasn't wrapping his arm around Gwen or Amaya, but what did that mean?

And if he didn't like me, why did I sometimes catch him staring?

The only thing he'd said was that he didn't do relationships, but I hadn't asked for one.

Nothing made sense, and even if I could gather the courage to ask him, it didn't matter when he always made himself scarce as soon as Gwen and Amaya got up to leave.

I was missing something, and I couldn't explain it, but dread sunk my heart. Nico was keeping something from me.

So when Gwen suggested we snoop in Sebastian's things to see what he was hiding, I said, "I think we should do it."

"Really?" Amaya turned to me with a shocked expression.

I shrugged and put down the magazine that I wasn't actually reading. "We should know if we can trust them. Caroline is definitely prejudice against darkyras, but she's still looking out for us. High priestesses stick together, and she's known him longer than us."

We didn't know either of these guys, and finding answers seemed like a good idea.

When Amaya asked how we'd distract Nico, Gwen's mischievous eyes ricochetted my way.

"Me?" I asked. Nico wasn't going to go for that, but I couldn't tell them why.

Gwen rolled her eyes. "He's obsessed with you. You'll tell him you want to go on a walk, and he'll jump up like a puppy with a leash in his mouth."

"He's not obsessed with me!" I countered. Most likely, he only hung out with me because he was a kind guy who knew how it felt to deal with a traumatic experience. "He's just nice. He understands...things."

There was nothing more to it.

"Yeah, and the other day you two were looking cozy cuddled together on the bed and practically jumped apart when we came in," Amaya teased. "That was obviously him being nice."

I stared at the ground, trying to make sense of the exact same thing.

***

Nico fell into our trap without any coercion.

For someone who had been avoiding being alone with me, he was really eager to go on a walk together.

I was lost in my head for the first couple blocks, guilt churning in my belly for tricking him. He really was just a nice guy. He was excited I was willing to leave the house because he thought it meant I was getting better.

In some ways, I was. I didn't flinch as the cars passed us on the street, and I hadn't had another flashback, but there were still moments I locked up, numbness leaving me frozen. The very thought of using my power made me shudder.

A blistering wind slammed into us as we got closer to downtown. I rubbed my hands together to fight the chill.

"Here," Nico said. He pulled out a hat and gloves from his coat pocket. "It's always colder than you think it's going to be down here. Something about the air flow between the skyscrapers."

"Thanks. You're sure you don't need them?"

"Nah." He pulled the hat over my head as I slipped on the gloves. "Soliser, remember? I run hot."

My bottom lip wobbled. He'd brought the gloves and hat for me then? His thoughtfulness made my chest ache, a sharp pain stabbing my heart. I rubbed below my collarbone, and his gaze followed my hand. Something dark passed over his eyes, but then he blinked it away.

"So, this is downtown," he said, walking backward and pointing out sights, pretending to be my tour guide. "And to your left is a smelly alley where drunk people piss. If you smell something pungent, it's our city's special concoction of dumpster garbage, throw up, and other bodily fluids that permeate the area."

I huffed a laugh. "Hey, your city isn't special. Pointedelle has that too."

"Ah, yes," Nico said. "But does Pointedelle have this?"

He fluttered a hand as we walked up to a bike rack.

"Bikes?" I chuckled. "Yeah. Believe it or not, we actually do."

"Not just any bikes." He brought out his phone and did something that made two of the bikes unlock with a beep. "Fae powered bikes."

I raised my eyebrows. "What?"

He pulled the bike out and brought it around for me. "Okay so, unfortunately, to get them to work you have to take your gloves off because the skin of your hand needs to come into contact with this metal part right here, see?"

The handle bars had a rounded metal plate on top and wires that connected to a box in the middle of the bike.

"You give it a bit of your power—it doesn't take much at all—and then the motor is juiced up," he said.

I chewed on my lip. A sour acid stung the inner lining of my stomach. I didn't want to explain to Nico why I couldn't summon my power. I didn't even want to think about it myself.

He noticed my hesitation. "It's pretty cold, so how about you keep your gloves on, and I'll charge this one for you?" He placed his hands on the metal.

"Thanks," I said in a small voice, not meeting his gaze.

"No problem. What are soliser friends for if not to keep ya'll warm?"

Friends.

Right.

Because that's all we were.

I forced a smile that probably looked like a grimace.

He cleared his throat and stepped away from the bike. "There. That's more than enough to get us to the park."

He jogged over to his bike, and led the way to the bike lane.

I followed behind, pedaling to get started and then pressed the button to use the power in the battery.

The bike shot forward. I squealed from the sudden get-up-and-go.

Nico's deep masculine laugh echoed behind me. "Takes a light touch!"

"Now you tell me!" I yelled back, but the chastisement was undercut by my giggling.

My heart raced as the cold air lashed my face. Adrenaline-induced giddiness warmed me, replacing my gloom.

Nico continued his impromptu tour of the city, hollering over the wind.

He showed me where Daria's bar was and the place with the best bagels, along with the restaurant he had a gift card to from the girl who slashed his tires.

Each new fun fact about Palagui City was accompanied by a smile thrown over his shoulder as he checked that I was keeping up.

I'm pretty sure we took the scenic route to the park because it felt like we'd biked all over the city. We returned the bikes at a different rack and started strolling through the park.

Kids shouted in excitement as they chased each other on a playground, and there was a hum of chatter from the sidewalks. People bundled up in puffy coats queued at a food cart. The park was in the middle of it all. Roads and skyscrapers lined the outskirts.

We crossed over a little pedestrian bridge, which overlooked a stream. Nico's hand bumped into mine; tingles fluttered through me despite my skin being shielded by a glove.

Sitting on a bench near the water, we watched a kid who was flinging pieces of bread to the ducks.

"Do you want kids?" I asked, and then sucked my lips into my mouth.

Oh boy.

Here I was saying I wasn't asking for his hand in marriage, and now I was asking him about whether he wants kids? I was probably pumping out some kind of clingy pheromone that he was reacting to.

No wonder he didn't want to kiss me.

"Yeah," he said, lounging and stretching his arms on either side of the back of the park bench. "I love kids. I work at a school."

I shrugged and chanced a look at him. He didn't seem upset by the question. He was watching the kid with the ducks too.

"Well, yeah," I said. "That could be the exact reason you don't want them. Because you have to deal with them every day. What if you have kids like Rollin and George?" The troublemaking kids, who starred in many of Nico's stories.

He snorted and crossed his legs at the ankle. "My kids will be nothing like them. My kids will be cool as shit."

The corner of my lip crept up, picturing a little boy and a little girl with his auburn hair and big smile.

"What about you?" His voice shifted in octave lower.

"I want a big family," I said. "Lots of little ones."

His eyes brightened. A warm joy effused from him, heat radiating even through our jackets. His happiness hovered around us, like his aura was a golden sparkling light, the sun catching and bouncing off it.

My chest squeezed tight. The ache in my heart increased, making it hard to expand my lungs for a full inhale.

"Sloane, there's something I—"

Bang. A car backfired, and the high-pitch squeal of tires pierced my ears.

I gasped, my body tensing as panic quickened my heartbeat. The warmth that surrounded me shifted from comforting to claustrophobic. Flames ripped through my skin. I couldn't scream as smoke from my charred skin mixed with car exhaust, choking me.

The burning, blistering pain was inescapable.

A hand grabbed my shoulder.

I whimpered, and it disappeared. I was relieved and aggrieved at the same time. It made no sense.

"You're on a park bench."

My vision was blurry. I couldn't contradict the voice.

"You're in Palagui. The sidewalk below our feet is gray. The lady to the right of us is wearing a red scarf." The fuzzy shape of a body crouched down in front of me.

My unseeing eyes blinked and focused on his face.

"What colors do you see, Sloane?"

I blinked again.

"What color is my coat?"

My focus steadied. "Black."

Nico held up my hands. "Good. What about your gloves?"

"Blue."

"Perfect. Tell me three things around us. Go."

My eyes darted around. He was blocking my view of the road on the other side, so I could only see the rest of the park. "Uh, there's a man walking a little dog on a purple leash. And there's a pigeon trying to eat a cracker that a kid in a stroller dropped. And..." I trailed off and stared at the male in front of me.

Nico nodded. "Good. You're doing so good."

My heartbeat ratcheted down as he held my hands and squeezed.

I took a deep breath and sighed it out.

"One more thing," he encouraged in a soft voice.

I blinked away my tears and gave him a watery smile. "I see a sweet, kind soliser, who—no matter how bad things are—can always make me feel like everything is going to be okay."

He inhaled a ragged breath. "Sloane—"

But I cut him off, putting my hands on his jaw and dragging his mouth to mine. His lips were warm and soft. The shock froze him for a moment, but then, he was kissing me back, his big hands cupping my jaw and the back of my neck, chasing away any cold, any fear.

His mouth worked over mine in short, stomach-flipping nips. The world spun underneath me.

I tried to deepen the kiss, licking the bottom of his lip and tangling my hands in his long hair, but he pulled away, retreating to the middle of the sidewalk.

"Nico," I said, standing, about to walk to him, but he held up a hand, halting me.

"Not like this. We can't."

"Not like what?"

"You...You aren't ready for this. We should go back. You just had a flashback and—"

"I'm fine," I said. "You got me through it. I'm okay. That wasn't some adrenaline heightened thing. You know I've been wanting to kiss you. You know I wanted to kiss you in my bedroom the other night, but you ran and have been avoiding being alone with me. Just tell me why."

He massaged his fingers into his eyes.

"You can't tell me you don't want this too…" But my voice was less sure now. "I know that…that you have to feel it? The way you look at me. The way you touch me. I'm not making this up, am I?"

"I…" He paced in front of the park bench, scratching his arms under his coat, looking everywhere but at me. "It's not about us. It's about Amaya and Sebastian—"

My head jutted back. "What about them? They aren't together."

Nico pursed his lips and raised his eyebrows.

I shrugged. "Okay, so they have some weird thing going on, but that's for them to figure out. It doesn't involve us…"

My stomach twisted. Why did Amaya's relationship always get priority over mine?

Wringing my hands, I chastised myself. It wasn't fair to think that. It's not like she knew about how I ditched August so it wouldn't disrupt our friend group. I knew she wouldn't want to be the reason Nico and I didn't get together either.

"We can agree to keep it casual," I said. "It doesn't have to affect our friend group. We can agree to keep our feelings out of it."

I didn't know if that was possible for me, but I could fake it.

I shrugged, feigning nonchalance. "It's not like we're going to be in Palagui much longer. Friends with benefits, and no one has to know."

I gave him what I hoped was a convincing smile, but he only cringed as if in physical pain.

He'd stopped pacing and itching to shake his head. "Sloane. No." His fists clenched, and his face tightened. "No. We can *never* be friends with benefits."

I blinked as his words assaulted me. The sureness in them. The absolute resolution.

The utter disgust.

I *had* been reading this wrong. This didn't have anything to do with Amaya and Sebastian. He just couldn't figure out how to get me to stop flinging myself at him.

"Wow. Okay," I said, feeling myself shutting down. I pushed off the bench and walked a few steps toward the stream so he couldn't see my devastation.

He grabbed my arm. "Sloane. Wait. You don't understand."

I held my elbows. "It's okay, Nico. I do understand. I'm sorry I kept trying to kiss you. I wasn't listening—"

"No! Sloane. Don't apologize. I do want to kiss you, okay? I want to kiss you so freaking bad." He opened the palms of his hands like he was telling me his deepest darkest secret. "But you're my—" He coughed, and then threw his hands up. "Fuck!"

"I'm your friend," I finished for him. There was sexual attraction between us, but he wasn't interested in taking that anywhere. I needed to respect that. "I know. You told me this. I should have listened."

He covered his mouth with his hand. "No. I mean—ugh! I can't be friends with benefits with you because I feel"—he cringed—"more."

I furrowed my brow. "More?"

He started scratching incessantly, ripping his jacket off and throwing it over the park bench. "I can't think when I'm this itchy."

I grabbed both of his wrists. His eyes widened. "I'm so confused. Tell me what you want, Nico."

He winced.

"Is talking to me really that painful?" I asked.

He sighed and lowered his head, crestfallen.

"You like me," I said. "You want me, but you don't want to act on it."

"Not that I don't want to," he said. "But I can't."

I nodded and dropped his wrists.

He couldn't do anything with me because he was loyal to Sebastian. He didn't want to complicate things for his friend.

He was a good person.

Wasn't that part of why I liked him? He was kind and thoughtful. He was a good friend.

But I wished he wasn't. Just this one time.

I stepped back and handed him his jacket. "I get it."

His eyes swiveled back and forth between mine, looking for something.

"Let's just go back." Amaya and Gwen had better be done snooping because I couldn't handle being around him after this second rejection. Or was it the third?

He liked me.

But not enough to do anything about it.

Not enough to risk his friendship with Sebastian.

And who was I to expect him to?

If he'd asked me to jeopardize my friendship with Amaya and Gwen, I'd tell him no freaking way.

Nico and I were friends.

And that was all we'd ever be.

Chapter Thirteen: The Redo

Tandem Read to Descend into the Void Chapter 13
Nico

Bash was putting me in a real bad spot.

As if our shitty bargain wasn't enough, he had convinced me to persuade Amaya into binding her powers so she could pass Xenos's test.

Bash hadn't been there to explain it to her or coach her through the binding process.

And he hadn't come back to let me out of our stupid bargain.

I hadn't been able to speak to Sloane since our walk. It was too hard to keep lying to her, and my bargain had shifted from just itching to excruciating agony, reviving the phantom pains of my old war wounds.

She knew I wasn't telling her the whole truth. She'd stared at me when Daria told everyone that soliser initiation involved transforming into our one true form.

"What's your true form?" she'd asked. It'd been the first time she'd even looked at me since our walk.

I couldn't speak. Couldn't tell her the truth. The bargain was starting to twist all of my words. If I told her I was a dragon—the very same dragon she'd seen in the research center—it wouldn't take long for her to figure out there was more to it.

The bargain wouldn't let me admit this to her. My magic knew when I was trying to find loopholes. I'd promised I wouldn't even imply what she was to me. I'd barely been able to tell her I wanted more. So much more. To be her lover. Her boyfriend. Her mate. Her everything.

I wanted her more than I could articulate.

So I kind of snapped when Bash finally came back to the townhouse after Amaya bound her powers. My anger was smoking and clouding my thoughts. I couldn't understand anymore why he was doing this to us. To all of us.

"You should have been there!" I yelled at him as he held vigil over Amaya's unconscious body.

"I know. I know. Don't you think I wanted to be?" he asked, miserable. "I couldn't risk being near her after what happened between us."

I shook my head. "You need to tell her what's going on. It's only going to get worse."

If he just told her, we'd all be better off.

"No, it won't. Now that her shadow is bound, she'll be safe," he said.

I clenched my fists, fighting the urge to shake him until I could knock some sense back into him. "What's the plan? She's going to live life without her power? Because that worked out so well for you."

"It might work out for her. And if it doesn't, then she'll be initiated, and I'll stay away from her. She can go back to living the life she deserves."

"And me?" When was he going to let me out of this bargain?

"Your situation is completely different," he said. "You can open the gift you've been given. My gift is pandora's box. Only suffering and agony are in store. Even if I knew she wouldn't get hurt, I'll never get out of the bargain I made with them."

I sighed because I'd forgotten about that. It wasn't only his own stubbornness preventing them from being together. He'd made a bargain with the Darkyra Deity that he wouldn't attach himself to anyone.

There would be no accepting the mating bond between them.

The bedroom door opened, and Bash jerked away from Amaya as Sloane came rushing in.

"Oh Goddess, what happened to her?"

"She'll be okay," Bash said as he exited the room and disappeared.

Sloane glanced over her shoulder and glared at me. "This is your fault."

My eyebrows pulled together. "Sloane, I'm sorry, okay?"

I was sorry for so much. Not just for what was happening to Amaya, but for everything. For rejecting her. For not telling her the truth. Everything.

She shook her head. "I can't do this with you now."

I knew a dismissal when I heard one and left the room as Gwen barreled in with Daria.

I stomped my way down the hall to Bash's room and didn't bother to knock as I let myself in. He was nursing a glass of scotch and sitting on the chair beside the bar cart.

Another glass had already been poured. I sat across from him.

"Are you back for good?" I asked.

He nodded.

Well, that was something at least.

He leaned forward with his elbows on his knees, holding his head. "I don't know what to do, Nico."

I sighed. For all my annoyance and anger with him. He was in an impossible situation.

"I know I'm messing things up for you, and I know our bargain isn't fair." He looked up. "She can't know. Not yet. Especially now. Without her power..."

"You have to tell her."

He rubbed his temples. "I will."

"Sloane hates me," I said. "This bargain isn't just about the mating bond. I can't even tell her I like her as more than just a friend."

"You agreed to a poorly worded bargain."

I threw my hands up. "Story of my life. Reckless decisions got me here, but I'm asking you to amend it. We'll keep the mating bond a secret for now, but you can't stop me from telling Sloane that she's more than a friend to me. That I love her."

His eyes darted to mine.

"Don't look at me like that. You love Amaya too. You know it or you wouldn't be doing all this."

He slumped over, like the truth being spoken aloud crushed him.

I grabbed his shoulder. "Come on, buddy. After you come clean to her, you can tell her why you can't accept the bond, and she'll understand. She was asking about you while you were gone. She feels it too. There's got to be a way you can be with her without accepting the bond."

"She will never forgive me for what I did."

"She'll understand why you couldn't tell her about the bond right away."

Bash looked up. "Not about that."

My hand slipped from his shoulder. Oh. The draxis.

"You'll explain everything," I said, rallying a hopeful tone. "You'll tell her why you made the decisions you did, and she will understand. She's an empath. She'll feel your sincerity."

"Right," he said quietly.

We sat in silence as he finished the rest of his drink, then he stood, his eyes looking upward and flicking side-to-side as he thought.

"Okay," he started. "I agree to negate our prior bargain and make a new bargain to allow you to tell Sloane what she means to you as long as you don't use the word mate, mates, or imply the mating bond."

I jumped up and clasped his hand in both of mine, shaking it quickly before he had a chance to change his mind. "I agree."

The magic wasn't as strong as the last time, but the static of the energy raised the hairs on my arms as it settled in my sternum.

Bash slapped a hand on my arm. "Go get the girl, Nico."

Grinning, I sprinted to the door.

I needed to find Sloane. I needed to tell her I liked her. That I loved her. I wanted to grab her, pick her up, and spin her around. I'd kiss the shit out of her and then tell her that I wanted to be her boyfriend. I wanted to take her on dates. I wanted to wake up beside her for the rest of my life. I wanted—

"Maybe apologize first," Bash said. "Ease into it so you don't overwhelm her?"

I skidded to a halt at his door.

Oh. Yeah.

He was probably right.

"And don't fuck her," he said. "They'll figure it out if their powers grow."

I nodded and shot him finger guns as I calmly left his room.

There would be no kissing and spinning and declarations of love.

Not yet.

I'd gotten into this bargain so I'd take things slow. Just because I could now admit what I was feeling didn't mean Sloane was going to be ready to hear it.

Not after I rejected her in the park.

I sighed and went to my apartment. I needed to think about how to go about this and not impulsively rush ahead.

I didn't want to be too much.

Chapter Fourteen: The Healing

Tandem Read to Descend into the Void Chapter 15
Sloane

Healing wasn't linear.

I had spent days in a numb stupor, unable to focus or find motivation to get out of bed. I was moping a little about Nico, but more than that, I realized that I'd let myself be distracted by him as a way to escape and dissociate from what was happening inside my head.

The days that I'd been flirty and happy, when my only worry was trying to figure out what a boy felt about me, those days had been my band-aid. A way to ignore the wound festering underneath.

But the flashback in the park, Nico's rejection and odd behavior, plus Amaya's bound powers, it all reminded me of the truth of my situation.

Whatever progress I'd thought I made crumbled away. I didn't know who I was anymore. In Delnee, I was Sloane Knight, a high priestess who worked at the surveillance agency with the power to sense high priestess powers and heal.

I was the girl that flirted and dated around in an attempt to trick myself into believing that my life would fall into place if I just found *the one*. I sat at my desk at work and fantasized about being a field agent, going on high-stakes missions to save people and kick butt.

I imagined romantic scenarios and adventures because if I couldn't choose the direction my life took, I could at least choose what life I lived out in my head.

But I couldn't use my power since my kidnapping. And I didn't have a dramatic or romantic story to escape into anymore.

I was stuck living with the truth. I was a broken shell of who I used to be. I had no choice, no say, nothing to live for.

For a few weeks, that was how it stayed. Nico was around, but I couldn't bring myself to say more than a few words to him, to anyone.

It only started to get better when Gwen forced Amaya and me into the backyard for training. Amaya got hurt, and without thinking, I'd raised my hands to heal her.

The white light trickled from my palms, easy and familiar.

My chest expanded on an inhale like the gasp of breath after having been drowning. I'd been so afraid of using my power, but when someone I loved was hurt, my instincts had taken over.

And nothing bad happened. In fact, tapping into it rejuvenated something inside of me.

Amaya and I still spent our days indoors, but something shifted. Something that couldn't have been uncovered if I hadn't sunk to rock bottom. A little window of hope that the rest of my life didn't have to be this way.

By healing someone else, I remembered that it was worth trying to heal myself too.

Chapter Fifteen: The Partial Truth

Tandem Read to Descend into the Void Chapter 17
Nico

I hated going to court. I hated that Sloane was here even more. My skin prickled, licks of heat in my veins that told me my dragon was antsy. I didn't want my mate anywhere near these vindictive people. They cheered for humans' deaths and reveled in Bash's emotional pain. Their viciousness hung heavy in the space, coating the entire top floor of the court building in depravity.

But we needed to get Sloane's citizenship papers notarized, and Bash and Amaya needed to fake their way through the engagement ritual to keep up their ruse for Xenos, so here we were.

"Is this where your typical weekend is spent?" Sloane asked as her eyes darted around, taking in the chaos.

I scrunched up my face. "Goddess, no. We don't come here unless we have to."

I stepped to the side so that I was blocking the girls from the rest of the room, thinking maybe I could keep them from the courtiers' prying eyes.

Sloane hummed. "So where do you usually go out on the weekends?"

My dread momentarily fell away, a weight lifting and my spirit animating. Sloane was finally talking to me again!

We hadn't been on the best terms lately. Despite that I could now tell her how I felt without choking on my tongue or my skin breaking out into hives—I couldn't figure out how to break through the wall she'd built after the disaster at the park.

I couldn't figure out how to tell her I wanted more without explaining what had changed.

"Daria's bar, The Cave, is where I like to hang out," I said, beaming.

"Her vigilante bar?" Sloane asked.

I bobbed my head faster, excitement rising. "Yeah, I could take you there next Saturday if you want."

Panic widened her eyes

Too much, I scolded myself. *Too fucking much.*

"I mean, we could all go," I revised. "We might even get Sebastian to come since Tilted Haze is playing."

Sloane bit her lip but smiled. "That could be fun."

"Cool. Cool," I said, trying to tamp down the giddiness. This was basically like a date. She agreed to go on a date with me.

Sloane agreed to go on a date with me!

Well, sort of.

A group date…okay, a group outing. But still. It was something.

Hope pinballed inside of me, bouncing around and threatening to erupt into dancing or singing or falling to my knees to praise the Goddess.

I forced myself to stop fidgeting and cleared my throat. "We should go get your papers notarized while we're waiting so we don't have to stay here longer than necessary." I turned to Amaya and Gwen. "Will you two be okay by yourselves?"

They nodded. The gossips would have a field day after the engagement ritual, but if they stayed here, in the corner, until Bash got back, they hopefully wouldn't catch anyone's attention.

A worried furrow knitted Sloane's eyebrows together.

Amaya waved a dismissive hand. "Seriously, we'll be fine. Get your papers."

Reluctantly, Sloane nodded. I gestured to the lobby door, and she followed.

My inner dragon demanded I place my hand on her back, or partially shift so my wings could cover and block her from everyone. I shoved those urges away.

We walked down the corridor to the offices and backrooms. A voluptuous female in nothing but pasties and a thong walked by. Her breasts and the flesh around her stomach and hips jiggled as she met my eye.

I inclined my head toward her in greeting.

"Hey, Nico," Angie said.

"Hi, Angie."

The male with his arm around Angie's shoulders smirked. "Nico," Vince said, his voice impassive. "I didn't know you and Angie were acquainted."

Angie perked up. "I gave him a lap dance a few weeks ago."

"What?" Sloane shrieked. She tried to hide her reaction with a cough.

"It wasn't like that," I whispered to her.

She pressed her lips together.

"Don't worry, darling," Vince said and tucked Angie closer. "Angie's a *professional* dancer. Nothing untoward would have happened."

Angie rolled her eyes and lightheartedly bumped her hip with Vince's. I fought the urge to grimace. Just the sound of his voice made me want to gag. I didn't know why Angie was so playful with him.

"In fact," Vince said, leaning in to whisper in Angie's ear, still loud enough for us to hear. "I think you owe me one of those dances tonight, don't you, sweetheart?"

Angie hummed, not particularly enthused, but neither was she upset.

Vince winked at me and escorted Angie down the hall.

"Who was that guy?" Sloane asked after they'd turned the corner.

"Vince. He's the soliser scumbag that was elected to the council to represent Merbany."

"Oh." She was silent for a beat as we continued down the hall and stopped in front of the notary office. "I thought you didn't come here much? Just when you feel like getting lap dances, I guess."

Was she jealous? My power fizzed in my core. Mentally, I was throwing my fists in the air in delight. She still liked me enough to get jealous.

"It wasn't like that," I said. "Xenos gave her to me. Bash and Amaya asked for a pleasure slave too. Just ask her. I kept my hands in respectful places and gave Angie the rest of the night off as soon as Xenos left. It was all fake."

She pursed her lips.

"If it makes you feel better, it was the worst lap dance I ever got."

I was only half joking. I'd never have guessed Angie was a professional dancer. She was clumsy and danced like she had no clue what she was doing. Maybe it was just nerves.

Sloane's face pinched. She crossed her arms over her chest. "Is that the kind of girl you like?"

I tilted my head in confusion. "What do you mean?"

She waved her hands, making an hourglass shape. "Curves and..." She shrugged. "A real female. Is that why you didn't want—" She cut herself off and blushed, looking at the ground.

I closed the space between us and grabbed her chin, tilting her face to mine. My hand was as big as her head, taking up the space from her jaw to her temple. "Make no mistake, Sloane. I only have one type. *You*. You are my only type. You're the most beautiful female I've ever seen. What happened a few weeks ago had absolutely nothing to do with a lack of desire. I want you so bad it physically hurts."

My heart lightened. Goddess, it felt good to be able to say that.

Her eyes fell. "Right, but Amaya and Sebastian..."

I curled her short blonde hair around both ears and stroked my thumbs along her cheekbones. "You were right. Whatever they're doing is their business. I'm tired of denying what I want. I can't stand the space between us, and I haven't been able to figure out how to close it."

Her gaze met mine, hope sparkling in her eyes. "What are you saying?"

"I like you," I said, choosing the smallest word to describe what I felt. "I think you're amazing and smart and beautiful. You make the fire in my veins burn hotter. I'm sorry it's taken me this long to figure out how to say it. Can we forget about what happened at the park? Can we start over?"

"Nico," she said on a heavy sigh.

"I want to kiss you," I blurted out.

Her eyes fluttered shut as if she was no longer in conscious control, as if her body was reacting to mine.

She whispered my name and leaned on her tiptoes. I crushed my lips to hers, immediately deepening the kiss like I'd wanted to in the park, like I'd been dreaming of doing since the moment I saw her.

Her hands slid up my chest, grabbed handfuls of my shirt, and pulled me down. My tongue swept through her mouth, and she made a sexy little moan that I was sure I'd hear echo in my mind for the rest of my life.

My power flared to life. My cock did too. The pulsation of need throbbed throughout my body. I pressed her into a closed door, wanting all of my body to touch all of hers.

She was too short though. I was leaning down to grab her ass, to lift her until we slotted together, when someone cleared their throat behind us.

I ripped my head away from my mate, about to growl and probably throw a fire ball, but the notary was looking at me with a pinched expression, tapping his foot.

"Oops," Sloane said. She wiggled herself free and fixed her hair.

I took a deep breath to cool the blaze of my lust. I managed to settled down my inner dragon enough to open the door to the office.

The notary didn't waste any time. Maybe he was uncomfortable with the way Sloane and I were staring at one another like we wanted to rip each other's clothes off.

As she signed the last document, I said, "You're a Palaguian citizen now. How's it feel?"

She could stay in the country. She could stay here with *me*.

Sloane smiled. The first genuine smile I'd seen from her in a long time. "Feels like a fresh start."

Chapter Sixteen: The Cave

Tandem Read to Descend into the Void Chapter 20
Sloane

I could sense fae powers now. All fae powers. Not just high priestesses.

My power had expanded.

A lot.

I started noticing it the day after we went to court and Amaya was almost killed by Sebastian's ex, Jeremy.

The trauma and adrenaline of thinking my best friend was going to die must have triggered my power increase, or it'd increased after I'd been kidnapped and I hadn't noticed until I started using my powers again.

Those were the only explanations I could come up with.

Amaya's near-death experience rocked all of us. Changed everyone's focus and energy. I knew it. I could feel it.

I still needed to touch someone to sense their power, but it wasn't as hard as it used to be to tap into the core of their life force.

When I sat shoulder-to-shoulder with Gwen in the evenings, the hum of her power vibrated through me like a steady, even buzz. A manifestation of the honed and focused energy she had been cultivating since she started working on some project for Caroline and the council.

When I cuddled up next to Amaya as we watched TV in bed, the chill of her shadows tickled the underside of my skin. It was like I could feel sounds, even though I didn't hear them. Hers was a high-pitch ding that reminded me of a piano out of tune.

When I brushed against Sebastian in the hallway, I felt the echo of that same piano note. It must have been a darkyra thing.

And when I kissed Nico…

It was unlike anything I'd ever experienced before.

The air was heavy, sparked with static, but I was weightless. Every strand of my hair floated in space; I was floating. He touched me, and his power moved through me. If everyone else's power was a whisper, his was a symphony. A concert hall full of singers, their songs echoing and harmonizing in a perfect melody.

His mouth would move against mine, his tongue licking and twining with mine, devouring me in brutal and possessive kisses. He always started slow, but it didn't take long for his control to snap, for his sweet caresses to turn into hungry squeezes of my hips, my butt, my thighs. His heat, his touch, his taste were so intoxicating that I'd devolve into a melted puddle of goo.

We hadn't gone further than heavy petting and making out. Mostly because I hadn't told Gwen and Amaya about what was happening and I didn't want them walking in on us. Something about what we were doing felt fragile. A part of me was worried that if our friends knew, Nico would change his mind about me.

But if—or when—Sebastian and Amaya officially got together, then our relationship wouldn't need to stay a secret either.

Ever since Amaya almost died at court, the energy between her and Sebastian had intensified, and Amaya had developed a new determination to get him to let his guard down.

"Is it against bro code if I ask what's going on between Amaya and Sebastian?" I'd asked Nico one evening while we were in the kitchen making dinner.

Nico stirred the sauce at the stove. "I think it's pretty obvious, isn't it? Doesn't take an empath to know they like each other, and he's being an idiot about it."

"Oh, for sure, but why?"

Nico pressed his lips together. "It's not really my place to say."

"Sorry. I wasn't trying to pry. I just want them to be together is all." I shrugged, wondering if baking my infatuation cookies, as Gwen called them, would put good vibes into the universe for them. "Maybe we should lock them in a room together or something until they figure out their problems."

Nico raised an eyebrow. "You want to play matchmaker?"

"Maybe," I said, elongating the word.

Nico smiled deviously.

***

The pulse of the bass thrummed through the crowd, its vibration traveling up my body as I danced next to my best friends in Daria's bar.

I knew our matchmaking plan had been a success when I saw dark hair and blue eyes lurking behind us. Gwen had already gone to get some water, so I made an excuse about going to the bathroom.

"You stay here," I told Amaya when she asked if I wanted her to come with me.

I knew Sebastian wouldn't be able to resist her all dolled up and dancing.

I giggled to myself and squeezed my way through the crowd. Gwen was leaning over the bar, talking to Daria. I let them continue their flirtation and went to freshen up in the restroom.

When I came back out, Gwen and Daria were no longer at the bar. I scanned the place for them while typing out a text.

"They went to the supply room in the back," Nico said, holding a drink and tilting his head toward a hallway.

I raised my eyebrows. "Like to...?"

Nico shrugged. "I have no idea. Daria isn't really one to blow off a shift for a quickie in the closet, but who knows?"

I tucked my phone away. "That's more your style."

"Why put off enjoyment for later when you could have it now?"

I put both of my hands on my hips. "Why, indeed?" It was more a challenge than a question.

Nico looked handsome but casual in dark jeans and a gray V-neck shirt, his arm muscles threatening the integrity of the soft fabric. He'd elected to leave his long, wavy auburn hair down tonight. My fingers itched to touch it.

He stepped close enough that his chest was pressed to mine. "Do you want to keep dancing, Sloane?"

I pressed my bottom lip out. "No...my feet hurt." It was a lie, but I kicked my foot up and looked behind me to indicate my heels.

Nico's gaze lingered on my legs and backside as he hummed. "Those do look painful..." His eyes met mine. "But damn, do you look good in them."

I grabbed his shoulders and leaned up on my tiptoes, my mouth by his ear. "You know what's my favorite outfit to wear with them?"

"What?" he asked, breathless.

"Nothing," I whispered.

He groaned and grabbed my hips, pulling me close to him so I could feel him thickening in his pants. The heat in his eyes made promises for what was in store for me tonight.

Someone from the crowd called his name.

Nico cursed under his breath as he turned around, his hands never leaving my hips, positioning me in front of him. No doubt to hide what was going on below the belt.

A dark-haired male with several scars on his face pushed through the crowd to get to us, or more like the crowd parted for him because his presence was more than a little intimidating. Based on the broadness of his shoulders and height, I pegged him as a soliser.

"Mateo," Nico said. "How are ya, buddy?"

Mateo glanced at me. "I'm getting by. Who's your friend?" He took a swig of his drink.

"Sloane, Mateo. Mateo, Sloane."

Mateo's eyes widened. "Thee Sloane? The girl you're obsessed with?"

Nico scoffed. "Shut up. I'm not obsessed."

Mateo huffed a laugh. "Yeah, okay. I scored a table over there." He gestured with his drink. "You guys heading out or do you wanna join me?"

I waited a beat so Nico could politely decline his friend, but instead he said, "Yeah, sure. Lead the way."

A sinking disappointment settled in my stomach, but I forced a smile to hide it. Maybe he was just being nice to his friend.

Or maybe he didn't want this as bad as I did…

If that was the case, I'd have to try a little harder to make sure he was sufficiently motivated to get out of here.

Nico interlaced our fingers and tugged me through the crowd after Mateo.

The table only had two chairs. Mateo sat in one, and before Nico could be chivalrous and offer the other to me, I waved a hand toward it. "You sit. I'll sit on your lap."

Nico grinned, and his arms came around my waist as I made myself comfortable on his thighs.

Mateo watched us with a faintly amused expression, and I leaned forward—maybe wiggling my butt a little on Nico in the process—and asked Mateo, "So how do you two know each other?"

Nico answered for him, "Mateo comes to my school and tells me how to do my job better, and he used to"—Nico pushed his friend's shoulder—"come down to the practice ring at the gym, but I haven't seen him in months."

Mateo cringed. "Got a second job. Been taking up my evenings and weekends."

"Really?"

Mateo nodded but didn't elaborate. He took a long pull from his drink.

"So you work at the school too?" I asked, trying to ignore the way Nico's fingers were stroking my bare thigh at the edge of my dress.

"Sorta. I do freelance for the Education Administration. We oversee the programing for all the schools in Palagui and help create the training curriculum for solisers. Nico was actually the one that got me the job. I'd definitely never have gotten in without him."

"Pssht, yes you would have," Nico said. "You're an expert in soliser technique."

"Maybe theoretically, but my inability to wield fire would have made them skip right past me if this guy"—Mateo threw a thumb at Nico—"didn't sweet talk the recruitment lady."

"I didn't sweet talk her!"

"You did," Mateo said. "She still talks my ear off about *my charming, handsome friend who works in the Brookline North District.*"

I giggled. "Nico does have a way with people. Makes everyone his friend. Did he tell you about the girl who slashed his tires?"

Mateo waved a hand. "Yes, exactly! Who does that? Befriends the person that slashes their tires?"

"She was a nice girl," Nico protested. "And there are plenty of people who don't like me."

"Name one," Mateo said.

"Caroline? Gwen?" he said.

I shook my head. "Doesn't count. They don't like anyone."

We stared at Nico while he squinted, looking off into the distance.

Mateo threw up his hands. "He can't even think of one!"

Nico rolled his eyes. "Okay, most people like me now. But trust me. I was on a lot of people's shit list when I was younger."

"Why?" I asked.

He shrugged, his face serious. "I couldn't always control my anger. My fire was pretty reactive for a long time."

I was about to press him for more information, but my phone buzzed, and I pulled it out to see a text from Amaya with an address and a shadow emoji.

I tilted the screen so Nico could see.

He snorted. "He's pulling out all the stops and taking her to the beach house."

I widened my eyes. "He has a beach house?"

"Oh, yeah," Nico said. "It's real nice."

"Huh," I said and texted a bunch of emojis to tell her I knew *exactly* what was going to be happening at that beach house.

Gwen texted a thumbs up, but when I scanned the bar again to see if she'd come out of the back room, I still didn't see her or Daria.

Strange.

But at least she was okay.

I slipped my phone away and leaned over the table. "So I wanna hear the most embarrassing stories you have of Nico."

Mateo finally cracked a full smile.

"Wow. Look at the time?" Nico said, standing us both up. "It's been fun, but Sloane and I actually have to get going to...you know—anywhere but here."

"Come on now—" I was cut off as Nico pulled me away. Mateo waved goodbye as we were swallowed by the crowd.

"It was nice to meet you!" I called out.

The crisp night air was a relief after being squished by people to get out the door. Nico pointed to a car, idling in front of the bar.

He opened the door to the backseat and offered his hand as I slid in, his thumb brushing my palm and sending shivers through my body.

"Where are we going?" I asked.

"Home," he said, smiling. "I called the car as soon as you came off the dance floor, but it's been a busy night. Took them this long to get here."

My stomach flipped in giddy anticipation.

He *did* want this as bad as I did.

Chapter Seventeen: The Toys

Sloane

I'd been in Nico's apartment a few times before when he'd gone to grab something. It was very plain. A small kitchen and living room, which were connected to a bathroom and bedroom. No decorations. No knick-knacks. No personality. No trace of his vibrant aura hovering in the space.

He went to the fridge and handed me a bottle of water.

"When did you move here?" I asked, taking a swig.

He twisted the cap off his water. "After I came back from the war."

I nodded, doing the math. "So you've lived next to Bash for like thirty-five years?"

He grinned. "Yep. I really just sleep here. I spend most of my time in the townhouse. Bash pretends to be annoyed about it, but he's never asked me to move out, and I'm too stubborn to take any of his moods seriously."

"Is there anything you take seriously?" I joked.

He put his bottle on the counter, angled his body toward mine, and took my water, setting it aside to hold my hands. "This. What we're doing here, Sloane. This is real for me. I know I joke around a lot, but I'm taking this relationship very seriously."

I swallowed. An ache throbbed under my collarbone, my heart a magnet trying to rip out of my chest. "Me too."

He leaned down and pressed his lips to mine. My mouth tingled, the fire of his power blazed through my veins, making me soft and malleable under his touch.

His arms wrapped around my waist, and my hands found their way into his hair. I twisted the long, wavy auburn strands around my fingers, holding him to me, pressing my body into his.

He kissed me gently, gingerly, soft little pecks that had me panting for more. I tightened my grip and tugged on his hair.

"Nico," I sighed. His mouth trailed teasing little kisses down my neck, sparks zinging. His sweet, smoky scent filled my senses.

"How do you want me, Sloane?" The question was whispered into my neck as his teeth nipped and mouthed at the sensitive skin under my ear. "Do you want me gentle? Do you want me rough? What do you like?"

I shook my head, a moan escaping as he sucked a trail down my neck, eliciting a pleasurable hollowness that it felt like only he could fill. A deep thrum in the core of my belly tugged. "I don't know. All of it. Any of it. Just you. Just want you. Anyway I can get you."

His breath hitched, and a ring of orange flared around his irises, but I only saw it for a moment because then he was on me, crowding me down the hall and against the wall. His kisses lost their gentle, teasing touch as his tongue plunged into my mouth, exploring, making my clit throb with need. My entire body heated up, melting into him.

With my mouth fused to his, I scrambled to get under his shirt, brushing against the soft hair on his stomach and up the trail to his chest.

"Nico," I murmured. "Off."

My delirious need had reduced me to monosyllabic words.

He reached back and pulled his shirt off, tossing it on the floor. I'd seen the bumps and ridges of his scars on his upper back when I slathered lotion on him in my attempts to flirt with him. There were lighter scars on his pecs and down the sides of his waist too. I traced my fingers along the raised skin and ran my lips along the scars, kissing a path across his heart and to the soliser tattoo on his sternum. A kiss for each of the four corners of the wavy sun, one on each pec, one at the notch where his collarbones met, one at the flare of his ribs.

He shuddered, and I leaned away, about to discard my dress when he fell to his knees and pushed my dress up over my hips. He peppered kisses on the thin triangle of fabric between my legs.

"Oh," I said, and my head fell back. His big hands grabbed my hips and held me captive against the wall. He ran his nose up and down over my underwear with just a hint of pressure on my clit, nowhere near enough, but my legs were still shaking.

"I've dreamt of this. Of what being between your legs would feel like. About what you'd taste like." He moved to place kisses right above my waistband. Flecks of orange melted into an almost gold in his eager hazel eyes as he looked up at me. "Can I taste you, Sloane?"

I ran my hands through his hair, scratching my nails into his scalp. "Please. Please."

His fingers hooked the sides of my panties and pulled them down my hips, baring me to his hungry gaze.

I stepped out of my underwear, and his hands ran from my ankles, along my calves, and up the sides of my thighs as he pressed his face to my pubic bone. His nose buried into the dark blonde hair between my thighs, breathing in my scent.

"Fuck, Sloane," he said. His knuckles turned white as he gripped me harder, palms so hot against my skin. And when his nose nudged my clit, the tiniest touch, my body jerked from the onslaught of pleasure.

I didn't know if I was going to make it.

My muscles were tweaking. My legs shaking so bad, collapse felt imminent.

I put my hands above my head, scrambling to find purchase on something, anything.

When I actually found fabric hanging above me, I gripped it as tight as I could.

Nico looked up and smiled. "What a great idea."

"Huh?" I said, lost and dazed.

"Pull yourself up."

I glanced at the bar hooked on the door frame. "I don't know how many pull-ups I can do in my current state…"

He chuckled. "Just need one. Hang on the straps."

I pulled myself up, and he wrapped my legs around his neck and positioned my thighs on his shoulders.

Oh.

I rested my upper arms in the cushioned slings that hung from the pull-up bar and held on to the straps. With all of my weight on Nico's shoulders, I didn't have to worry about my legs giving out anymore, but to stay in position, I had to contract my ab muscles for balance.

Rather than being distracting, clenching my stomach added a delicious tension, heightening the intensity of the warm desire pooling in my core. All of my power, all of my energy was concentrated, muscles firing and making me sensitive to Nico's every touch.

His arms encircled my legs, and his hands splayed out on my butt as he nuzzled his mouth between my spread thighs.

Sparks of his power sizzled against my skin and traveled through my veins.

He licked through my folds, and his tongue circled my clit in a maddening rhythm. He moaned, deep and low, a humming that rocketed through me as well.

The air was dry and alive with static energy, lighting up my body, raising the hairs on my arms, the back of my neck.

His mouth latched on to my clit, and his fingers teased my entrance.

My core quivered from balancing, increasing my pleasure and inching me higher. I was light and floaty, basking in the energy of his power.

"Nico," I said. "I'm so close."

And to my horror, he stopped.

"To coming?" he asked, looking up, almost slightly panicked.

I growled. "Yes. Yes. To coming. Nico. Please!" I squeezed his head between my thighs as if I could hold him there until he finished what he was doing.

"Sorry, Sloane," he said. I didn't know how he had the strength while kneeling and all my weight on his shoulders, but he stood, lifting me out of the hanging straps and putting me on the ground. My legs wobbled, and my chest flushed hot with frustration.

"What?" I wasn't going to cry, but I felt like I could. The abrupt shift was disorienting and vaguely sickening, like something had been snatched away from me.

"I made a very detailed plan on how this night would go, and we have to follow it exactly," Nico said.

I furrowed my brow. That was very un-Nico-like.

He didn't make detailed plans.

He certainly didn't insist on following them either.

Nico tugged my dress back into place over my hips, and then cupped my jaw. "You're important to me, Sloane. I don't want to mess anything up. I have to get it right."

My face softened as the frustration from the stalled orgasm faded away. I put my hand on the outside of his and pressed my cheek into his palm.

"You're important to me too. You can't mess it up. I promise. I just want to be with you tonight."

He kissed me, and I tilted my head, giving over to him and wrapping my arms around his neck. Lifting me behind my thighs, he carried me through the apartment, never breaking the kiss. I clung to him like he was the only light in my dark, dark world.

When he laid me out on the bed, there was a moment of uncoordinated undressing. We both tried to tug my dress off, but it was too tight, and I had to spin around so he could get the zipper.

Freed of my clothes, I indulged myself by rubbing my hands down his chest and squeezing his shoulders, his pecs, the thick barrel of his muscled chest and the mound of his stomach. He hopped on one foot and then the other, ripping off his jeans.

"Are you going back to what you were doing now?" I asked. "Or..." I shimmied farther up the bed, my eyes glued to the bulge in his tight red underwear, to the equipment that seemed more than proportional to this big, hulky male. "Or do I not get a say in our plan?"

"You get a say, Sloane." He grinned. "You get a say in how many times you want to come tonight."

"Oh yeah?" I raised my eyebrows. "I want to come all night long. Can you manage that?"

His grin twisted into a cocky smirk. "I promise you I can." Instead of taking his underwear off, he crouched down and pulled something out from under the bed.

I tried to catch a peek of what he was holding, but the bedroom was dim with only the soft glow of a lamp in the corner, and he commanded, "Lay back," before I could get a better look.

I did as I was told. He tossed something on the bed and crawled over me, his gaze devouring my body on the way up.

"You're so perfect," he said, both of his hands squeezing my small breasts. They were definitely not a handful, but from the way he was looking at me, I could almost believe he really did think I was perfect.

His hands ran down my ribs, and he bent over, licking and sucking my nipples, pulling a taut line through my body, the sensation like he was tonguing my clit.

My power trembled inside of me. His heat was burning through me, making me shake with need.

He kissed up my chest, over my collarbone, along my neck. I grabbed the back of his head and pulled his mouth to mine, intertwining our tongues. My legs wrapped around his waist, and I used that position to grind on his hard length.

He panted into our kiss as my hands snuck down to push off his underwear, but he caught my wrists and pinned them.

I whined, but he sat back between my legs and grabbed the stuff he'd tossed beside me.

"What—" My eyes widened at the little purple silicone C-shaped toy in his hand.

He grinned. "Spread your legs."

I widened my thighs, liking the heat of his gaze on my most sensitive parts. His thumb spread apart my folds and lightly traced along my entrance, gathering my wetness on the toy. He eased one part of the toy inside me and positioned the other side to rest on my clit.

"Do you think you can handle orgasms all night long?" he asked.

I narrowed my eyes. "You're cheating—" The toy must have been remote controlled because a vibration jolted me. It pulsed low and slow, stimulating my clit and my g-spot at the same time.

"Cheating? No. I don't think so." He leaned down and kissed my hip bone. He clicked off the toy, and my clenched muscles relaxed. His hands gripped under my thighs and spread my legs further apart. "I'm still the one giving you the orgasms, so it's not cheating."

I moaned in response as he turned it on again.

He laid out on his stomach between my legs, head propped up on one of his elbows. "This way I get to watch every single twitch you make. I won't miss a thing."

Licking and nipping my inner thighs and circling my entrance with the tip of his finger, he grinned with feral delight, like I was his toy to enjoy playing with all night long.

"Nico," I begged.

He turned off the toy with the remote. "Yes, Sloane?"

I didn't like swearing. I didn't care when other people did it, but the words always felt strange in my mouth. But lying there, I tried to think of the dirtiest thing I could say that would make him give me what I wanted.

I licked my lips and said, "I want you to fill me with your big cock and fuck me so hard I won't be able to sit down without thinking about you."

His jaw dropped. "Goddess, Sloane. How can you be so sweet and so naughty at the same time?"

I ran my hands along my breasts. "Don't you want to give me what I want?"

He watched my hands as I tweaked my nipples and wiggled my hips as seductively as I could.

With a hard swallow, he grabbed himself over his underwear and shook his head. "I'll fill you up."

He repositioned himself between my legs and turned the vibrator back on.

I was going to come; my muscles clenched, the pleasurable tingling of the prior almost-orgasm reigniting.

"Nico, please," I said. I was so empty, the toy was hardly enough, but something cold and smooth traced up my entrance and sunk deep inside me alongside the C-shaped vibrator.

My eyes rolled into the back of my head. The juxtaposition between the cold glass dildo inside me and Nico's warm hands holding my thighs open overwhelmed my brain with pleasure.

"How's that baby?"

I mumbled incoherently as the vibrator hummed on, and he thrust the dildo in and out of me. My orgasm loomed in the distance.

"That's a girl," he said, his gaze ricocheting between my face and between my legs. "Look how good you're taking it. Stuffed full, aren't you?"

I was delirious with need, hallucinating from desire. That was the only explanation for why it felt like something warm and scaled had wrapped around my ankle. Why my vision went hazy and a dragon's tail was tickling up my calf, teasing my inner thigh.

My healing power stuttered, palms lighting up. The moan that escaped as my body shook from pleasure morphed into a whimper as the heat of Nico disappeared. The mysterious scaled tail vanished.

My muscles convulsed, orgasm wracking my body and petering out in little clenches of my abdominal muscles. I blinked away the disorientation, and refocused on the male beside me. He stroked my hip, staring at me in a way I'd only fantasized about. Intense longing and devotion swirled golden-orange in his eyes.

He rolled onto me, body covering and cocooning me with all his glorious weight. "That's one, Sloane," he whispered, teasing my ear with his breath, his tongue. "You ready to go all night, baby? How many more do you think you can handle?"

My moan was half-protest, half-excited anticipation. He kissed me into oblivion before turning the toy back on and making good on his promise.

Chapter Eighteen: The Next Morning

Sloane

I woke up warm and toasty, which was odd because I was usually always cold, especially in the winter.

Slowly, the memories of last night trickled back in, and I became aware of my very sexy heat source.

My back was plastered to Nico's chest, my legs intertwined with his, my butt nuzzled into his groin. A very enticing, but still hidden cock was pressed against me.

I wiggled to test if he was awake, and when his hand gripped my hip, desire pooled between my legs.

I flipped around and pressed my hand to the outside of his underwear, rubbing on his hard length.

"That feels good," he said, his voice thick with sleep.

"It'll feel even better when it's in my mouth," I said and pushed him to lie on his back.

He groaned but grabbed my wandering hands. "Sloane. We shouldn't do that."

I pouted. "Why? You gave me like eight million orgasms last night, I can't give you one?"

He winced. "I don't want you to think this is about sex for me. You mean more to me than that, and I want to prove it."

"Come on, you don't have to be celibate for me."

Something intangible prickled in the back of my head. The sensation that I was missing something.

I shook my head. There was no reason to be suspicious. He'd told me he was serious about our relationship. He was trying to be careful because he was afraid of messing up.

In contrast to his words, his hands found their way under my shirt (well, his shirt) and stroked the undersides of my breasts.

Sensing my opening, I rocked my hips a little. "You really don't want to?" I sighed dramatically and started to roll off of him. "Okay."

His hands squeezed my torso, halting my movements. "Maybe…Maybe just one time? One orgasm won't mess things up, right?"

The question seemed to be more for himself than me, but I answered anyway. "It couldn't possibly mess things up."

Part of me liked that this sweet, confident male was cautious with me. Like I was special and important enough to be cherished.

He bit his lip, but then nodded. "Okay. Okay."

I shimmied down his legs and pulled off his underwear. When I finally settled back into my position, I faltered as I took in the size of him.

"Holy smokes."

Nico chuckled. "Wow. That reaction is the best compliment I've ever got."

I knew he was decently sized. Obviously, Nico is a big guy, but this was next level. He was long and thick and had a mouthwatering vein running up his length.

Maybe it was good we didn't go all the way last night. I'd need to work up to this.

I curled my short hair behind my ears and got situated in between his legs. I grabbed him at the base and tried to plan out my attack. "You're going to have to sit tight while I get my bearings," I said.

Nico smiled down at me and put both of his hands under his head. "Take all the time you want, baby. I promise there is nothing you can do that I won't enjoy."

Oh boy. I really was a goner for him because even the underside of his biceps and the tuft of his armpit hair was sexy to me.

I liked the heft of him, that he wasn't all muscle and bones. The soft layer over his hard muscles. He made me feel petite and protected. It was a heady sensation having this big, powerful male weak for me.

I started with little licks at the head of his cock, working my way down the length of him to get him slick before taking him fully into my mouth. Once there was enough lubrication, I used my hand to stroke him while I sucked on the head and teased the underside with my tongue.

His stomach tightened, and his breath became erratic. Hooded and glassy eyes marveled at me.

"Just like that, uh, yeah. Just like that," he said. And I kept up the stroke and suck method.

I kept a steady pace, breaking to lick and gently suck his balls. His thigh muscles jumped under my hand at that. "Good?" I checked in.

"Uhhh huh," Nico said, his mouth parted, chest heaving. "S'good."

Pride swelled in my chest that *I* could reduce *him* to monosyllabic babble.

He palmed the back of my head, not pushing or pressing, just a heavy weight, a presence, like he needed to touch me.

As he got progressively tenser, I quickened my pace, but then his hand was on my jaw, pulling me away.

"Okay—" he said. "Okay, wait."

I sat up. "You don't want to come in my mouth?"

He blinked several times and seemed to be shaking himself out of a stupor. "No, uh, well." He muttered something under his breath and then asked, "Can I come on your tits?"

"Okay," I said and rolled over. He kneeled above me, and I stroked his leg as he jerked himself.

"Squeeze them together for me," Nico said. "Play with your nipples."

I cupped my breasts and thumbed the nipples like he said.

Actually, this was so much better than him coming in my mouth because I got to watch. Watch how he sped up and gripped himself harder than I ever would have. How his eyes were glued to my chest, my face, my body until the second they rolled back into his head, and his release fell over me with a sexy male grunt. Pleasure contorted his face.

He watched as his come ran down my breasts and pooled between them. "Fuck that's so hot. You're so hot."

After his breathing returned to normal, he bent over and kissed me quick before jumping off the bed.

"Stay right there." He darted down the hall, and I caught a glimpse of his toned naked butt before it disappeared.

"I'm not sure where you think I'd go," I called out.

He returned with a wet cloth and cleaned me up, tossing it on the ground after using it.

Crawling back into bed, he snuggled up, arm enveloping me. "You still smell like me."

"I should shower."

He pouted.

I laughed. "If I shower, then you get to dirty me up again."

He must have liked that idea because he hopped up, threw me over his shoulder, and took me to the bathroom.

We washed each other. Despite the fact that he was hard again and I was more than ready for our next round, we only showered. After getting out, we toweled off and fell back into bed. It was too early to be awake.

We fell asleep naked and tangled together.

A knock on the door startled me awake, and I peeked my eyes open to check the clock.

I hadn't forgotten that Amaya, Gwen, and I had to go to the airport to meet Rien, but darn it, I wished I could have stayed in bed instead.

I shook Nico awake. "I have to go."

"No," he groaned. "Stay."

"Amaya and Gwen are outside. We have high priestess stuff to do."

He sighed and released me. "Fine."

My heart tripped over itself, delighted that he seemed as enamored with me as I was with him.

Nico got up while I searched under the bed for my dress.

He started to leave the bedroom, his naked butt on full display.

"Wait! Put some pants on!" I yelled, a little too loud.

"Why?" Nico smirked. "Whoever is at the door knows we spent the night together."

"It's for your own protection. Gwen isn't all threats, you know, and I'd hate to see you lose your dick before I got to see it in action."

Amaya would have probably appreciated the full frontal, if only because I was going to have a hard time describing it without visual representations.

Nico pulled on his underwear. "You very much so saw it in action."

I rolled my eyes. "No. Not in the way I really wanted to."

Another knock. I called out, "One minute!"

I finally got my dress zipped, and Nico went to open the door while I searched for my panties.

"Hey, Amaya." Nico's voice filtered down the hall as I scooped up my underwear and shimmied them on.

"Hey, Nico." Amaya said in a teasing tone. Oh, we had so much to talk about today.

"Sloane is getting dressed," he said, but he turned as I came into his peripheral, and when I tried to slip past him, he grabbed my waist, pulled me close, and kissed me.

As his lips worked over me, I momentarily forgot anyone was standing in front of us.

Amaya cleared her throat. "Should I come back later?"

"No," I said, shoving down the part of me that was protesting our separation.

"Yes," Nico said at the same time.

I bit my lip to hide my smile and grabbed Amaya's hand, dragging her down the stairs with me. "Bye, Nico."

I couldn't help but turn back to get one last look at him as we got to the door. The corner of his mouth quirked up, and my heart throbbed in longing.

Chapter Nineteen: The Betrayal

Tandem Read to Descend into the Void Chapter 25
Sloane

The highest highs and the lowest lows of my life had always occurred in back-to-back procession. I was given the lead role in our school play—the greatest thing to ever happen to me at the age of eight—and that night two high priestesses in uniform showed up on my grandmother's doorstep with news that my parents had died.

Last night with Nico had been life changing.

I wanted to dissect it, to turn it over, and discuss it with my best friends, but Gwen was in a bad mood and Amaya was distracted with texting on her phone, so I spent the tense car ride to and from the airport replaying every moment.

The intensity of my feelings for Nico surpassed any I'd felt before. This wasn't me being a hopeless romantic, in love with the idea of love. I had a bone-deep surety about Nico. There was a part of me that resonated with his presence, and it had nothing to do with the future. When I was with him, I wasn't living a fantasy concocted in my head. I was living in the present and...in love with it.

In love with him.

I was in love with Nico.

The highest high of my life.

Which meant it could only be accompanied by a crushing betrayal.

Worry had begun gnawing at me when Gwen announced we were making a pit stop to help Daria fight a draxis.

Gwen surprised Amaya and me when she admitted that she'd spent the night before killing draxis with Daria, and I didn't get a chance to express my anger with her because something much worse took place.

Amaya's face had paled to a deathly white as she stared at the draxis we'd captured and the spy chip that fell from its back. The same spy chip that had been planted in her room. When she'd confronted Sebastian about the equipment the night before, he'd told her Nico had created it.

Standing in the middle of the road, staring at the broken spy chip on the ground, we all came to the same realization.

Sebastian was tracking and controlling the draxis.

And Nico was helping him do it.

The agony of his betrayal made my knees weak. Fear and anger and confusion took over the love and bliss coursing through my veins. The throbbing in my heart turned from longing into a festering wound of resentment and humiliation, which was only made possible because I'd let Nico fill in the hollow spaces in my heart.

The highest high accompanied by the lowest low.

Chapter Twenty: The Ghosting

Tandem Read to Descend into the Void Chapter 32
Nico

"Are you fucking kidding me?"

Bash just shrugged and grinned.

I threw my hands up and paced the length of the balcony outside Bash's bedroom. "You told me we couldn't fuck them because they'd figure it out if their powers grew!"

He shrugged again. "I know. I know, but I mean...come on. I didn't, for a second, think you'd actually listen! The bond...I mean, there's no resisting the bond."

"There's. No. Resisting. The. Bond?!"

He rubbed the back of his neck and smiled down at the concrete floor.

"I think I might actually throw you off this balcony."

"You really didn't sleep with her?" he asked.

"No! I had it all planned out. I made sure we weren't touching for any orgasms."

He squinted his eyes, trying to figure out how that was possible.

"Toys." And I jerked off on her tits this morning, but he didn't need all the specifics.

He hummed, impressed. "I should have thought of that."

I ran a hand down my face. "This is so unfair."

He ignored my whining and stared off in the distance, his stupid grin never leaving his face. "I think you're right. I think maybe this could work out."

My shoulders fell, and I sighed. It was impossible to be annoyed with him when he was so happy.

"So you're negating our bargain? We're telling them?" I asked.

"Not yet."

I sighed. I should have known better. He insisted we talk on the balcony outside in the cold because he didn't want Amaya to come home and walk in on our conversation.

"I'll do it after the engagement party," he continued. "I'll take Amaya to your cabin and tell her everything. I'll make her understand."

That was only a few days away. I could do that. I'd been keeping the secret for this long. A few days was nothing.

"You swear?"

"Yes," he said. "As soon as the engagement party is over, I'll let you out of the bargain."

"Okay. Okay. Good." I clapped a hand on his back. "I'm happy for you. Amaya is an empath. She'll understand. She'll get it. Sloane says she really likes you."

"Yeah?" He beamed like a boy in grade school hearing his crush liked him too.

"Yeah," I said. "This will work out."

I pulled out my phone and texted Sloane. I couldn't resist. I wanted to know if she was thinking about me. About last night.

Nico: I tried to go back to sleep after you left but couldn't. My bed was too cold without you.

Sloane: Lies. You are made of fire.

Nico: It was a romantic figure of speech. I'm trying to woo you.

Sloane: My bad. *laughing emoji* Go on.

Nico: Dinner tonight? You and me?

Sloane: I'm not sure how long this stuff will take but sure.

Nico: Okay. Let me know. *heart emoji*

But she never did.

Dinnertime came and went, and I started getting worried.

When I heard a car pull into the driveway, I sprinted down the stairs.

Gwen slammed the door and practically snuck into the townhouse. She came back out, sans car keys, but she didn't get much farther because I blocked her path.

"Goddess!" she said. "You're a big lumbering giant, aren't you? Shouldn't someone your size make noise when they walk?"

"Shouldn't someone your size not insult someone my size?"

She sneered. "I could take you, fire breather. Now get out of my way."

"Have you seen Sloane? She isn't texting back."

Gwen glared. "We're doing important high priestess things. Things you don't need to know about."

My shoulders slumped.

Well, at least she was okay.

"Can you ask her to text me? I was just worried. I'm not trying to interrupt what you're doing."

Gwen put her hands in her coat pockets and popped her gum between her teeth. She gave me an unimpressed once over. "Sure thing. I'll get right on that the second I see her."

I sighed. Yeah, I bet she would.

Shadows appeared, and Daria stepped out.

"Hey, Nico," Daria said, but she didn't glance at me. I didn't think anything of it because her eyes were glued to Gwen. Where they always seemed glued.

"Hi, Daria," I said and left them in the backyard.

It wasn't until much later I realized it was weird that Gwen, Sloane, and Amaya were doing high priestess things with Daria, who was most definitely not a high priestess, but I couldn't voice my question because Sloane and Gwen didn't come home that night.

The next morning, I cornered Amaya as she snuck out of Bash's bedroom to ask where Sloane was, but I got no answers from her.

Just because they were doing high priestess things didn't mean Sloane couldn't shoot me a text. My twenty messages were starting to look a little lonely in the texting app. That's not counting the five voicemails I'd left last night.

Sloane not being around, not knowing where she was, made my dragon spin out. I burnt scald marks into my kitchen floor from the pacing I'd been doing. My back itched near my shoulder blades where my wings would sprout from. I caught myself about to shift three times. My dragon needed to fly, to find her, to bring her home.

Three days and two burnt-through punching bags later, I got her final message.

Sloane: I can't do this with you. This is all too much. I need space. Stop texting me. Stop calling me. I'm blocking your number. Don't bother trying to reach out again.

Nico: Why? Please just tell me why.

I put my phone down, and almost smacked myself in the face with it when it pinged again.

Message undelivered.

But she said why, didn't she?

My twenty text messages glared back at me. I'd done it again.

I was too much.

Too fucking much.

***

Bash had gone through the portal, so I hadn't been able to talk to him about what happened until he got back.

"Something is going on with the girls," I said. "They haven't come home. I think they've been staying with Daria."

"I sensed Amaya at the Hollow when I came out of the portal," Bash said. "She probably went to unbind her powers because I specifically told her to wait until after the engagement party to do so." He rolled his eyes but was smiling nonetheless. "Stubborn female," he muttered.

I shook my head. "And Sloane and Gwen? Why haven't they come home?"

He shrugged and scrolled on his phone, shopping for what looked like floor-length dresses. "Gwen is probably shacking up with Daria."

"Sloane basically broke up with me over text!"

He put his phone down and narrowed his eyes. "Why?"

I pushed my tongue into my bottom lip. "I don't know."

"What was the last thing you said?"

I sighed. "We were talking about getting dinner, and then she didn't come home, so I texted her. Three days later, she broke up with me!"

Bash put out his hand.

I reluctantly gave him my phone, and proceeded to fidget for the next few minutes as he read.

"Nico..." he said.

"I know, okay? But I was worried."

"Does the bond hurt?" he asked.

"No more than usual. Actually, a little less since we spent the night together," I said.

"The bond would hurt if she was in danger. I think..." He handed me the phone back. "You went a little overboard here."

I rubbed my eyes. My texts were all the explanation anyone needed.

"You don't think maybe they found out?" I asked. It'd been something I was considering. "It would explain Sloane's sudden change of heart."

Sebastian pursed his lips. "Or she got overwhelmed by your freak out and asked Gwen and Amaya to stay at Daria's with her so she didn't have to face you."

I deflated. "How could I have messed this up already?"

Bash frowned. "I'm going to the Hollow to wait for Amaya. If she's acting weird or out of sorts, maybe your theory has merit, but we can't really know that this isn't just..."

"My screw up."

"A minor speed bump," he said with a stern tone. "I'm sure Gwen and Sloane will be at the engagement party for Amaya. Just be cool and talk to Sloane. Apologize. After you tell her about being mates, maybe that'll help her understand that it wasn't your fault for freaking out. Give her time and space to make up her mind."

***

It'd been a great plan.

But the greater the plan, the more chance I had to screw it up.

"Sloane, please, let me explain," I said as soon as I spotted her at court in the main room.

Sloane's eyes widened. She scanned the room like she was looking for an escape.

"Just five minutes. Please. I can explain, and then, I promise I'll leave you alone."

Her gaze settled on me, sharpening into a glare. "I don't want your explanations. I want you to go away."

"It's not my fault. It's the—"

She put her hands on her hips. "Oh, really? That's what you're going with?" She shook her head. "I don't want to hear your excuses, Nico."

"Pleas—"

"Nico? Do you have them?" Bash's voice came from behind me, and I turned.

"Yeah. Here," I said and gave him the cuffs he asked me to bring.

"Can you take these to Amaya in the bathroom?" Bash asked Sloane. She took the fae cuffs and all but sprinted across the floor.

"Not going well?" Bash said.

"They know," I said, staring at the bathroom door that Sloane disappeared behind.

"No, they don't. Amaya didn't say anything—"

"They know."

He sighed.

"Let me out of the bargain. Now."

He wouldn't meet my eye. "I will. I will. I just need to get everything lined up—"

"Forget it," I said and threw a dismissive hand behind me as I walked away. He wasn't going to let me out of this bargain. He might never let me out of this bargain.

But Sloane needed to know the truth. If she wanted to leave me, then fine. But she was going to have all the information to make that decision.

So I'd do the only thing I could.

I'd break the bargain.

And the consequences could be damned.

Chapter Twenty-One: The Declaration

Tandem Read to The End of Descend into the Void
Nico

It was too much. *I* was too much, but I wasn't going to let her get away without explaining the truth.

She'd disappeared around a corner, but I closed my eyes and sensed into the place that her power and our bond dwelled in my heart. I opened an office door and found her rummaging in a desk.

Just being in her presence was a relief. My dragon's restless energy downshifted into a nervous tension. The urge to snatch her up and fly away was still strong, but I shoved it down as I followed her around the office and tried to explain, tried to lead her to the truth without saying the words.

I still wasn't sure if I'd be able to trick the bargain to get them out of my mouth.

I couldn't let my mind linger on what I was going to do. Couldn't let my brain toss around the word I wasn't saying.

"I know you feel it too," I said to Sloane. "The agony that burns in your chest when we're not together. The bliss that ignites when we touch." I couldn't resist running my fingers down her arm. The need to touch her was too strong to overcome. "My power burns brighter, hotter when I'm with you. You're the source. My fire, my heart."

I thought, maybe, by the softening in her eyes, I'd gotten through to her without breaking the bargain, but she only tried to sidestep me.

"I can't do this with you," she said.

"Sloane, you can't walk away from this. You and I are—"

But I was interrupted by the door creaking.

Sloane and I hid in the closet as Caroline and my father walked in. We listened to Caroline outline how she planned on betraying the girls and imprisoning Bash.

Sloane burst from the closet the second Caroline left.

I berated my father for his involvement, but Sloane was already pulling away toward the door.

"I need to save my friends," she said.

I grabbed her hand and swept her into my arms, tilting her chin so she'd see exactly how serious I was. I emptied my brain of everything and focused on Sloane's face.

"We'll save our friends together," I said. "You're my mate and I will not let you run blindly into danger." Her body trembled. "Not without me by your side."

A sharp pain ripped through my core, but I gritted my teeth through it. Sloane and I sprinted out of the office and around the corner, just in time to watch guards drag Amaya and Bash out of the ballroom.

Maybe it was the shock of seeing them, lifeless in the guards' arms, or the bargain needed a few minutes for the reality of what I'd done to sink in, but my magic burned a vengeful trail of pain through my body, weakening my limbs. My vision spotted, and I leaned on Sloane as I tried to swallow my agonized scream.

Still, I didn't regret a thing.

Chapter Twenty-Two: The Reconciliation

Sloane

Mate. Mate. Mate.

The words played on repeat in my head. I had a mate! Me. The hopeless romantic in me was skipping and dancing and bursting into song.

The other parts of me—the rational parts—knew there would be no celebration.

I'd considered ditching Nico, finding Gwen, and making a plan to save Amaya.

But when Nico's body collapsed into mine, when my heart twisted from the pain that my mate was in, I knew that ditching him had never really been an option.

We searched court for Gwen, waited for her at the townhouse, but when guards showed up at the door looking for her too, we figured she was also hiding from Caroline.

We barely managed to shake the guards, and in Nico's condition, we couldn't keep evading them, so we packed what we could and went to his cabin near Molbridge.

Nico explained through gritted teeth that he'd made a bargain with Sebastian to not discuss the mating bond. He explained how he helped

Sebastian collect high priestess powers through the draxis to keep the queen alive. And without him, it was only a matter of time before all of Palagui lost their powers when the queen died without crowning a new female.

My stomach churned with anxiety over Amaya's and Sebastian's imprisonment, Gwen's disappearance, and Nico's pain.

"I'm sorry, Sloane," Nico had said. "I'm so sorry. I'm sorry for lying to you. For getting you and your friends into this. You don't know how sorry I am. I love you so much. Please forgive me."

I'd never been one to hold a grudge—that was more Gwen's territory. To me, it always felt like more work to hold on to my anger.

Plus, the broken bargain was putting him in so much pain that I didn't have it in me to hold on to any resentment.

After he explained everything and apologized, I forgave him.

I loved him. Of course, I forgave him.

If we were going to save our friends, we were going to need each other.

And my heart knew that it would need him until I took my last breath.

"Promise no more lies?" I asked.

He nodded eagerly. "I promise. I swear. Do you want me to make a bargain?"

I chuckled and held his hand as I drove us to his cabin. "I don't think you should get into any new bargains while you're still paying for the last one."

He laughed, but the movement caused him to wince and clutch his side. "Probably a smart idea."

Chapter Twenty-Three: The True Form

Sloane

Weeks passed, and Nico's pain began to subside, which was good for us but very bad for Palagui.

"The queen is dying," Nico said. "I can barely conjure flames to light the fireplace, and I haven't felt my dragon's angst for days."

"Do we have matches—" I stopped and turned around from the stove to look at him across the island counter. "Wait. You have a dragon?"

He opened and closed his mouth. "Uh," he said, shifting back and forth. "Did I not tell you about my dragon?"

I crossed my arms over my chest and shook my head.

"Right. Well, I wasn't lying. It kind of slipped my mind that you didn't know."

I tapped my foot and tilted my head, using my wooden spoon to gesture for him to go on.

"Well," he said, pulling over a stool and sitting beside me as I stirred the soup. "I'm a soliser, right?"

"Right."

"And we all have one true form."

"So I've heard. Daria told me, remember? While you stood there mute."

"Right," he said. "You're not supposed to tell anyone your true form. If people knew that you could turn into a bird or a deer, then they can hunt down those animals and try to kill you."

I blinked.

"But that was, you know, back in the day. Nowadays solisers only shift into their one true form during initiation. It's the only time that we're able to call upon enough power to do so."

"Uh huh."

Nico got up and pushed the stool away, bouncing on his feet. "Except for shifters like me who can shift whenever they want."

I turned off the stove and stared at him. "When you say your dragon, you don't mean you have a dragon, you mean you are one?"

He beamed. "Yep!"

"So when Gwen calls you fire breather…"

He tilted his head. "Yeah, I guess I shouldn't have been so honest when I tried to trick her empath powers. It's just I'm not as good at lying as Bash is."

"So you *are* a purple-hearted dragon with the biggest—"

He waggled his eyebrows. "You can finish the sentence, Sloane."

I stared at his groin and shrugged. "It was definitely the biggest I've ever seen."

He snorted.

"So let me see it."

He smirked. "My cock? Pretty sure you already have. But by all means, I can show you again."

"No! Your dragon!"

His face fell. "I can't."

"Why not?"

"It takes a lot of power to shift, and with the queen dying, I don't have any to draw from. My ability to shift…" He grimaced. "It got messed up in the military. They gave us all these steroid enhancements to grow our powers. But you can't stop taking the

steroids once you start, so when I got captured as a prisoner of war…
The enemy barely needed to torture me, going through withdrawal
was torture enough. My powers never really recovered. I can still shift,
but it takes so long that I feel every bone breaking and bending into a
new shape."

"Oh…" I put my arms around his torso, gentle so I didn't squeeze
any sore parts. "I thought maybe…well, I've hallucinated you as a
dragon. Or at least the scales and maybe the tail?"

He rested his chin on the top of my head. "I know you have. It's
because you're my mate. You can see my true form. You see the real me."

"Your dragon self is your real self?"

He shrugged. "Sometimes it feels more real than my fae self."

"I'm sorry that you can't access it then."

He shrugged again. "It's okay. I could only do it when I was here at
the cabin anyway. Where I could be sure no one would see."

"So do you have a purple heart?"

"Nah. That was the lie. Pretty sure mine is the same color as
everyone else's."

I blinked. "Right. Wow. Okay. This is all a lot to take in."

He pulled back to look into my eyes. "Too much?"

I put my hand on his jaw. "No. Not too much. Just a lot."

He gave me a pained smile but nodded once.

Chapter Twenty-Four: The Bond

Tandem Read to Seize the Power Chapter 8
Nico

I needed to be careful, which was definitely not my middle name. I already almost lost Sloane once, or...like three times, actually. I couldn't mess up again. I could not.

Except, I did.

In my effort to try to contain my misery, to not be a burden or too much for Sloane to handle, I bottled up all the pain from the broken bargain and ended up exploding from frustration and helplessness.

When fae power started dying, the pain had become easier to manage as the broken bargain couldn't draw on my magic.

But that meant that I was blissfully unaware until the moment the bargain inflamed my old war wounds.

Magic wasn't stupid. It couldn't elicit the pain responses in me when it was weakened, so it used the memories of my torture and the phantom pains as retribution.

My war wounds, the craters carved into my torso and upper back, burned like they were freshly scraped raw. My legs weakened, and I collapsed to the floor for the second time that day. I tried to grab the counter for support but ended up taking my plate down with me. Chunks of scrambled egg flew all over the kitchen.

I grimaced as the pain ratcheted higher, and my weakness escaped as an angry growl. I picked up the plate and threw it at the cabinet, watching the pieces shatter.

Clenching my hands into fists, I tried to summon the strength to get up. I had to. I had to be stronger. I had to prove—

"Nico!"

By trying to cover up my pain, trying not to be too much, I pushed Sloane away. I screwed up.

Again.

I sucked at being a mate.

Sloane scolded me, rightfully so, for not telling her how much pain I was in, for not leaning on her when I needed it. She was so sweet, even when she was trying to be stern.

This wasn't the male I wanted to be. I didn't want to give into the pain and the anger. I didn't want to be the male who left his best friend to go to the military instead of talking about his feelings. I didn't want to be the male who came back more broken and damaged than when he left.

Sloane sat beside me on the couch, our fingers interlaced. I promised her to do better, and started to promise no more plate smashing...but it gave me an idea.

My bubbly, perfect mate was so full of love and joy. The last few weeks had been hard on us, harder still on Amaya and Sebastian, and Gwen, wherever she was.

But as Sloane yelled her war cry and brought the wooden bat over her head to smash the plates that we'd set up on a tree stump outside, it felt like I could finally breathe again.

My pain subsided, and the little bit of power that I had left flooded by body with adrenaline. Sloane's cheeks were flushed with excitement. I couldn't resist picking her up and spinning her around in the open field.

The bond pulsed between us. A faint purr of contentment from my dragon rumbled through my body.

"Accept the bond with me, Sloane."

She refused at first, afraid that the bond would increase our magic and, therefore, my pain.

But this was right. I'd been thinking about it for a few weeks now. We'd come up with a plan to break Sebastian and Amaya out of prison, and having more fae power between us would only help.

More than that, I wanted Sloane to know I was serious about our relationship. That despite my misguided lies and stupid bargain, I was always only ever thinking of her. I wanted to be bonded to my mate.

I wanted her forever.

I almost couldn't believe it when she said, "Okay, if you're sure."

I scooped her up and yelled my excitement until it echoed in the meadow. She giggled in my arms the whole way back to the cabin.

My dragon shivered as she said, "I want to accept the bond with you."

I tossed her on the bed and climbed up her body. "Yes. Fuck, yes," I mumbled into her neck as I kissed and licked her collarbone, her breasts. All of her was *mine, mine, mine.*

Our lips met, igniting the flames of my desire. She made a little noise that I swallowed as I grabbed her ass and guided her legs around my waist. Our heads tilted, mouths slotting together, tongues twisting and twining, ravenous for each other.

My power curled low in my belly, heating and trying to burst out, but the bargain's pain didn't latch on to the spark. Every part of my brain was zoomed into the narrow slice of Sloane's neck, and the lush curve of her breasts, and the dip of her collarbone.

Her hands were all over me, leaving a tingling trail of her possession on my shoulders, arms, down my torso. My eyes rolled back into my head, and I moaned as her hand slipped into my sweatpants and grabbed my hard cock.

She'd only stroked me for a few seconds before I had to stop her. "Sloane, your hand feels real good. Too good, in fact." I panted the last words out as I bent my head and buried my face into her neck. "And I kinda wanna be inside you when I come, if that's okay with you?"

She giggled and released me. "That sounds good to me."

"Excellent," I said and shifted downward, spreading her legs wide. "First, though..."

"Mmm," she said as I kissed her inner thigh, running my nose along the seam of her leg. The scent of her arousal filled my senses, but I held steady, teasing her with my lips and tongue and fingers.

It wasn't until she was writhing and whining my name that I finally pressed a soft kiss to her clit.

I tongued around the edges of the swollen bud, just little nudges. She grabbed a handful of my hair, and her thighs wrapped around my head, holding me in position.

My hands snaked under her legs, kneading her ass as I gave in to what she really wanted and sucked her clit. My hips started jerking unconsciously, rubbing myself on the bed. I had to stop. The friction on my cock and the way she was moaning and squeezing my head, suffocating me on her pussy, was going to make me come.

Luckily, I didn't have to last much longer. Her body tensed, and she cried out my name as the orgasm worked through her body.

She went limp, her legs splayed out and an arm thrown over her eyes.

"Damn, you work out or something? Pretty sure you could kill a male with those thighs," I joked, nuzzling into her neck.

She giggled her cute little giggle. "Sorry. Did I hurt you?"

"No, but if I am gonna go out, that's exactly how I wanna go."

She lightly slapped my shoulder. "*Squeezed to death while performing cunnilingus* is not going on your tombstone."

"Damnit, but all the other tombstones would be so jealous."

"Nico!" She laughed as we wrestled and rolled around on the bed until she was straddling me, pinning my hands above my head.

She was breathing hard and smiling wide. She blew out a breath to push her short blonde hair from her eyes.

"Changed my mind," I said. "This is how I want to go out."

"How about like this?" She released one of my wrists and reached between her legs and positioned my cock at her entrance.

I sucked in a breath through my teeth as she slowly sunk down. I rested my free hand on her hip, guiding her as she took me into her body.

"Ah. Goddess. Yes," I muttered.

My eyes darted from the gorgeous sight of her pussy squeezing my cock to her face.

"Are you okay?" I asked.

"Mmhmm," she said, but her eyes were closed, and her face was a little tense.

"Sloane, we can stop if it hurts. We don't have to have penetrative sex to accept the bond."

"We don't?"

"Hell no. There are plenty of ways I can make you come. My dick is just one of them. As my mouth so expertly demonstrated five minutes ago."

She laughed—and *fuck me*—that laugh made her abs clench, and she squeezed me harder. She felt so incredible. Warm and wet and so fucking good.

"I want to though," she said, her eyes heating as she rocked her hips on top of me.

"Oh, fuck. Yeah, okay. Cool. You know, whatever you're into—" I broke off, at a loss for words, too mesmerized by watching her bounce on my cock.

She leaned forward and interlaced our fingers, holding my arms above my head.

"Sloane," I said. "I can't rub your clit if you got my hands pinned."

She ground down on my pelvic bone, so apparently, she had it handled. My body was hers to use as she pleased, and I was enjoying just being her fuck toy.

Her back arched, pressing her hard nipples close to my face. She made circles with her hips, getting herself off, using me. It was driving me insane. My mind emptied of thoughts. I was falling into that mindless, instinctual place that I went to when I shifted. There was no separation between me and my dragon anymore.

Sloane gasped. My vision was tinged orange. I hadn't fully shifted, but my tail wrapped around Sloane's thigh and was rubbing against her clit as she pulsed her hips back and forth on top of me.

Her hands released my wrists and ran down my torso, over the wavy sun tattoo at my sternum which was shifting into orange and red and yellow glistening scales.

A wave of panic gripped me. Sloane's eyes darted around my body, taking in my partial transformation.

Her wide eyes softened into pleasure, and she gasped the words, "I love you. I love that I'm your mate."

Burning ecstasy melted the panic. I didn't have flowery words. Didn't even have the wherewithal to create a coherent sentence.

"Mine," I growled and wrapped my arms around her and flipped us until she was under me. "My mate," I said, my voice no longer my own but the animalistic rasp of my inner dragon.

"Yours," she promised. Sloane angled her hips and took me beautifully. Her fingernails dug into my shoulders as I thrust into her.

I kissed her, wanting every part of my body in contact with every part of hers. No, not just in contact, I wanted to be inside all of her. My cock, my tongue, my heart, all of it surrounded by Sloane's warmth.

My skin prickled, my scales extra sensitive as she brushed her fingers over my chest.

Our gazes locked, and at the same time, we both looked down to the place our bodies were meeting. Where my tail was playing with her, stroking and coaxing out those sweet little moans.

My body heated; the fire in my veins ignited. A flicker of flames turned into a raging inferno, overtaking everything as pleasure licked up my spine, and her pussy fluttered and squeezed my cock, milking my release from me.

"Nico," she sobbed. Her body shuddered as the orgasm swept through her. Her palms brightened with white light.

Our hearts merged, melted and fused together. The bond opened up completely as the boundaries of our auras fell. The echo of Sloane's orgasm hummed through my body, doubling, tripling my pleasure.

"Sloane," I sighed. I covered her body with mine, holding her as both of our bodies shook, and the bond solidified.

Chapter Twenty-Five: The Power to Heal

Tandem Read to Seize the Power Chapter 33
Sloane

Accepting the bond didn't fix all of our problems. As the bond strengthened our powers, it also intensified Nico's pain, and while I was beside myself with worry for days, after we made it to the prison to help Sebastian and Amaya escape, Nico was finally free of the broken bargain.

We spent the next few months helping our friends navigate their new jobs as Queen and King of Palagui. I let that task distract me from the existential dread that settled into my bones when I thought about my future.

I knew that my fantasy of being a field agent was just that—a fantasy I'd used to escape my dreary reality in Delnee.

But knowing what I didn't want to do didn't help me figure out what my next steps were.

At least, in Delnee, where everything was planned for me, I could complain about my job at the Society without the expectation that I could change my circumstances. There was a safety in that because here, in Palagui, I had no one to blame for being unfulfilled other than myself.

"Do you think I'd be a good healer?" I asked Nico a few days after Sebastian's healing ritual with Karina. The entire process had been so intriguing. It'd lit up some part of my brain that hadn't been used before.

Nico furrowed his brow. "You're already a healer. You heal people all the time. You just healed my knuckles the other day when I went too hard at the gym."

I shook my head. "I mean an actual healer. Like if I went to school for it and did it professionally."

"Of course! You'd be good at anything you try."

I looked at my palms. "Right."

But did that mean there might be something out there I'd like even more than healing then? Something else I was supposed to do with my life? I wished I had a road map or some way to see into the future.

Nico and I were baking—what would Gwen call these? Not infatuation cookies—distraction pastries, maybe. I put my head in my palm and watched Nico bend over the counter and squeeze the filling into the shell of the pastry roll. He'd been so excited to show me this recipe, and the distraction was mostly working.

Mostly.

"So what do you see yourself doing in the future? Do you think we'll keep living in the apartment?" I asked.

He snorted. "Has Gwen gotten to you? Don't tell me you also think I'm mooching off Sebastian."

"No," I said. "Nothing like that. I mean, have you ever thought about getting your own place?"

He shrugged. "Not really. I don't like thinking too far into the future."

"Oh, okay," I said.

"Do you want to move? Cause I'd do whatever you wanted. I figured you liked being near your friends too?"

"Yeah," I said. "I do. Just thinking out loud."

I didn't know how to explain that I didn't know how to make a decision because I'd never had a choice that required me to make one.

I went to the only high priestess school in Delnee.

I lived with Gwen because she was my best friend.

The High Priestess Society gave me my job in the surveillance office.

I wouldn't have had a say in who I married or had children with. It would have all been determined by the Society.

Oh sure, I'd decided what dinners I made and what people I danced with at the clubs, but those were minuscule compared to deciding what direction to take my life.

I could do anything I wanted in Palagui.

Anything.

And I was paralyzed by my endless options.

***

"What underpins everything we do is connection," Karina explained. "The healing center itself benefits from connection. Molbridge holds community rituals every month, which charge up not only the individuals participating but the very ground we stand on."

Amaya convinced me that doing an internship at the healing center would be a good idea. I'd been observing Karina and other healers for the past few days.

"If you'd like, you can assist me in a healing ritual today," Karina said. "We'll step into trance, and from that position, you'll be able to tap in and feel what I'm doing with my power."

"Really?" My face broke out into a grin. "Are you sure I can? I don't want to hurt anyone."

Karina put a hand on my shoulder. "Think of it more like I'm recruiting your magic. I'll hold the container of healing, so you can't possibly hurt anyone."

I took a breath to steel myself. "Okay. Yes!"

Karina had already gotten the patient's permission for his treatment to be used as a trainee demonstration.

Our patient, Seru, was a bitter-looking soliser. He scowled through the opening grounding ceremony and only responded to Karina's instructions with a grunt.

But it quickly became apparent his body and mind were in turmoil.

Karina and I stood above Seru. My hands rested on his left shoulder, hers on his right.

I let Karina's magic sweep through me, and it unlocked the barrier around Seru.

I couldn't see inside his mind; it wasn't visual, instead I stepped into a different plane of existence where I had a sixth sense. Some combination of feeling energy and seeing light and just knowing where the power dwelled.

On my first day, Karina described the anatomy of healing. "Fae power travels through the body along the fascia, which has a bioelectrical current that sometimes gets blocked. We use our power to stimulate the fascia and encourage it to loosen. Unlike when our high priestess power stimulates tissue repair, we can't force the fascia to release. The harder you try to do that, the harder the blockage becomes to untangle. We try to make the patient as comfortable and relaxed as possible so they don't inadvertently make their condition worse by tensing."

I'd seen the healing process from an outsider's perspective as a participant in Sebastian's ritual, but being a co-creator in the healing energy was exhilarating.

My hands warmed, and my body tingled as energy filled me and flowed into Seru. I felt his fascia, the sticky, gummy webbing that lived under his skin and held all his organs.

My fingers twitched as my magic traveled through his body. I sensed I was near the liver, but I had no idea how I knew that. There was so much anger, so much tension.

The webbing here was thick and dry.

Intuitively, I used a bit of my energy to nudge it. The fascia didn't react. I imagined a salty ocean wave, gentle and roaring, flowing over the area.

Seru flinched under my hand, but then his shoulder slumped in relaxation. His fascia bounced a little when I poked it again. It had a little bit of give to it now.

I must have pressed too hard the next round. An image flashed behind my closed eyelids. No longer was I a healer helping Seru, but I *was* him. Rage curled sour in my stomach. Flashes of fists, of pain, of groups of people yelling, of fire, of hatred.

I scraped back the thick, crusty fascia, and underneath held overwhelming helplessness and insecurity. Righteous anger hiding fear and grief. A life spent looking over his shoulder, preparing himself for the next attack or attacking before anyone else had the chance to.

The heat of his anger flooded my body. Or was it my anger?

Karina broke through the rush of feelings and said, "Emotions cause the release of neuropeptides, which are the chemicals in our brain that communicate with the cells of our body. Our emotions change the electrical frequency and chemistry we emit. His power is trying to talk to you. Tell it what you'd like it to know."

I took a deep breath to focus my power. Digging inside myself, I felt into the warmth of my core, imagined holding a peaceful ball of light and becoming a conduit for positive energy.

The magic spilled out and scattered throughout myself, Karina, and Seru.

I couldn't recall the rest of the ritual. I let myself float in this other plane of existence, being the conductor, aligning the energy that flowed between us.

Karina grounded us and brought the ritual to a close.

Seru didn't seem as healed as some of the other participants had been after a treatment. He was neither energetic nor blissed out. He simply thanked Karina and I both and quietly left.

"Did I screw it up?" I asked. "He didn't seem...fixed. The fascia around his liver was still not completely healed."

We started cleaning up the chairs and straightening the room.

"Seru has been coming here for several weeks," Karina said. "He has some chronic issues as well as a history of abuse. I won't get into the specifics, but the fascia around his liver was as healthy as I've seen it in a long time. You didn't screw anything up at all."

"Oh."

"Seru is someone who would benefit from a summer solstice ritual—something to connect him to the natural world—but until then, we do the best we can for him," she said. "I should have probably asked this before, but can you sense fae power?"

I nodded as we stacked up the last chair.

"Makes sense," she said. "I haven't seen anyone locate the fascial disruption as easily as you did. You're a natural energy healer."

My skin tingled with an equal measure of excitement and anxiety.

Maybe this *was* what I was meant to do.

"What is the process of becoming a professional healer?" I asked.

Karina smiled. "Well, it's a long one. You'll need to take entrance exams to get into medical school, and then..."

She outlined the numerous steps I'd need to take. Years of schooling and interning and then residency and on and on. With each additional task, I felt a band constricting tighter around my chest. Deciding on a career was a huge commitment.

Just because I had an interest in healing didn't mean it was what I was supposed to do. What if I changed my mind? What if I chose wrong?

An infinite number of paths laid in front of me, and I had no idea which direction I was supposed to go.

Chapter Twenty-Six: The Future

Tandem Read to The End of Seize the Power
Sloane

"It makes sense that you're confused," Gwen said as we sipped sparkling wine at a High Priestess Society Gala in Delnee.

I'd come to Delnee to tell my grandmother I was moving to Palagui, and she'd immediately peppered me with questions.

What are you thinking?

What are you going to do there?

What are you going to do with your life?

Palagui isn't safe. You can only trust the Delnee High Priestess Society. They know what's best for us.

Telling her that I'd found my mate had only made her scoff. *He's not your mate. Young love can just feel intense sometimes, but that doesn't mean you throw away your life.*

I didn't doubt Nico as my mate or my safety in Palagui, but I didn't have a good answer to her other questions.

"The Society screwed us up," Gwen continued. "They told us we could have potatoes or bread for dinner. Then we bust out of Delnee and find out there is a whole damn buffet out there! It makes sense you're going to gorge yourself. You're going to try things and see if you like them, and eventually, you'll find your favorite food, but you can't beat yourself up for not picking the perfect meal on the first go around."

At the time, I'd nodded my agreement and let her advice bounce around in my head.

But there was nothing like being taken hostage by your best friend's aunt and used as bait for your other best friend's crown to really underscore that your mundane life choices weren't actually life-or-death.

After Amaya killed Caroline, and we took the SoCo terrorists to the fae prison, my career drama paled in comparison.

Gwen's advice made sense. I didn't have to make the *right* decision because there was no such thing as right.

Healing Amaya that day in the backyard had been the catalyst to pull myself out of my depression. Using my power to heal Seru during my internship was thrilling, and for now, that was the path I was following.

If I changed my mind, or found something else I liked more, then I could reassess, but it didn't mean I had to regret my past choices. I was following the path that seemed like the most intriguing challenge.

Karina offered me a position as her assistant while I studied for medical school entrance exams. Nico got a job transfer, and we moved to Molbridge.

I didn't know if my job was forever, or if the house we were living in was forever, but it felt good, and that was all that mattered.

I think our battle at the research center also put things into perspective for Nico too. He became very insistent that we make plans for our future.

Our family's future.

Not just our jobs or where we'd live, but plans that included having little ones with auburn hair and hazel eyes running around.

We agreed to wait a few years to settle down together, but I was already scrolling through baby names on my lunch breaks.

And we wouldn't be raising our kids alone. Amaya had already made her status as *best auntie ever* clear, and for all that Gwen can't stand adults, she was actually really good with kids. Something about their emotions being simple and solvable.

Plus, after the almost-war with Delnee, I convinced my grandmother to move to Palagui. She stayed with us for a few weeks, and then, we set her up in an apartment near the ocean. I think the sea air was doing her good.

It took a while, but she finally accepted that Nico was my mate.

She could still be a little judgmental and old-fashioned though, which was why I planned a trip to the cabin with Nico after we had dinner with her that evening.

Our visits to her house always made Nico anxious. I could see the way he shrunk himself down the second we walked in the door. How he'd catch himself with a slap to the thigh when his knee started bouncing. Or how my grandmother would scold him if he started tapping his fork on the table when he was telling a story.

By the end of the evening, my bright and joyful mate was zapped of all his zest.

It broke my heart.

"So," I said as we climbed into the car after dinner. "I have a surprise for you."

He tried to smile, but it was vacant and lifeless. "Yeah?"

"We're going away this weekend."

He furrowed his brow. "We are?"

"Yep! We're going to the cabin. I already packed our bags and got all the supplies."

Nico blinked and turned around to see the backseat was stuffed full. "How did I not notice that when we got in?"

I waved my hand. "You kinda miss a lot of obvious stuff."

His eyes darted back to mine, and a genuine smile spread across his face. "Did you pack the bat?"

I gave him an incredulous look. "Of course! And Amaya, Sebastian and Gwen are sifting in tomorrow evening."

"Fuck yeah," he said and shifted the car into reverse and peeled out of the driveway.

I grinned and squealed as his excitement caught the spark of mine and ignited. The car took a sharp turn, and the tires screeched.

His face fell, and he pulled the car over to the curb. "Sloane. I'm so sorry. Are you okay?"

I tilted my head in confusion. "Yeah? I'm fine. You weren't going that fast, and I had my seatbelt on."

"No. The sound. The tires. You…"

"Oh." My head jutted back. "Wow. I didn't freak out. I guess that sound isn't a trigger anymore?"

"I'm so glad." He grabbed my hand and kissed the back of it. "Still, I'm sorry I did that. I just got excited. I know I can be too much." He shook his head and tensed his body as if he was trying to contain all of his energy.

I frowned. That wasn't the first time Nico had said something like that. Apologized for being himself, for his enthusiasm. Sure, sometimes he was a little scattered, but he could always focus on the important stuff when it came down to it.

I grabbed handfuls of his shirt and tugged him close. "Who told you that you were too much?"

His jaw fell open. The vulnerability in his eyes had my power churning, preparing to battle and defend my mate.

"Just…you know, people," he said. "I've always been this way. When I was a teenager, my fire manifested as anger. I'm better than I used to be, but my energy can still be over the top."

My heart sank for the younger Nico. The boy who had no outlet for the power coursing through him. His passion for working as a trainer at the school made sense, helping young fae harness their powers for productive rather than destructive use.

"I like your muchness," I said. "I don't want you to be any less than exactly who you are."

He became almost bashful. "Yeah?"

"In fact, my muchness needs your muchness. Whoever told you that you were too much obviously wasn't much enough. They lacked muchness!"

He laughed. "I feel like you've said the word much so many times it's losing its meaning."

"Good! Much much much much!" I grasped both sides of his face and gave him a big smacking kiss. "Much has no meaning now. You can erase it from your head. I've declared it no longer a word in our language."

He cupped my jaw and kissed me with such unbridled passion the windows started to fog up.

"I love you, Sloane," he whispered on my lips.

"I love you too, Nico."

Epilogue: The Dragon

Sloane

"I can't tell if you're nervous or excited?"

Nico was hopping back and forth on his feet as he looked outside the cabin window. Our bond was vibrating with energy, swirling like a hurricane.

"Both?" he said, rubbing his hands together. "My dragon is excited, but I'm...nervous."

I slipped on my shoes. "Well, if it still hurts, we'll try something else. This is just an experiment."

We walked out of the cabin and into the field. The grass had grown long, and wildflowers dotted the expanse.

Once we were far enough away from the cabin, Nico started taking off his shirt. I whistled and catcalled him, and he shimmied his hips, stripping like he was dancing for money.

I clapped my hands. "Take it off!"

He laughed, standing naked in the field. The joking had lightened his anxiety, but tension flooded back into his posture as he closed his eyes.

I closed my eyes too, sensing into the connection between us. Nico's magic intertwined with mine. His power, his warmth, his care, his kindness, it all held the tenderness of my heart in a comforting hammock.

The bond pulled taut, and my stomach swooped as he pulled magic from our bond and through the ether.

I focused on keeping our connection open, on relaxing and releasing. I recalled the techniques that Karina had been teaching me during our healing sessions, planting my feet firm to the ground but keeping my torso and shoulders loose to allow for the flow of magic.

Peeking my eyes open, I watched Nico transform.

The oranges and reds and yellows of his scales glistened iridescent in the sunshine. His body bent and snapped, shifting before my eyes in one fluid motion. His face and neck elongated, eyes and nose widening. His torso lengthened, and his hands and feet sprouted claws.

The dragon's eyes were still squeezed shut. A summer breeze rustled the grasses, and the bond prickled with a new kind of magic. Something ancient and wise.

I stepped toward the creature that my mate had become and placed my palm on his warm cheek. The dragon's body shuddered, and his tail flicked, finding my thigh and curling around it.

"You're so beautiful," I said, stroking his scaled face and his neck with reverence.

Not as beautiful as you are. I felt his answer more than I heard it. It wasn't like being sent Sebastian's or Amaya's thoughts, which appeared in my head in their voice. Talking to Nico in his dragon form was more second nature, a knowing that resonated through my body, something that I'd experienced in little muted bursts when we experimented with what we could do with our bond, but it'd been nothing like this.

Like this, he was pure magic.

"Did it hurt?"

The dragon shook his head. *Not as much as it used to. I think it's getting better. I think you really did it.*

I squealed in excitement.

My time at the healing center made me curious about how we could use our healing powers to heal different fae conditions. Nico's body suffered a great deal of trauma while he was a prisoner of war. His physical wounds were healed, and with the help of Karina and the healing center, he'd been able to work through the emotional and mental traumas that he'd suffered.

But his fae powers hadn't healed, not fully.

With Karina's supervision, I'd started experimenting on Nico, nudging his shifting magic with my healing power and our mating bond. It'd taken months, but slowly he felt something release.

It usually took him ten to fifteen minutes of agony to align his power and start the shift. One by one his bones broke and snapped and molded, scales regrew, organs transformed, but today he'd shifted in less than a minute.

If we continued the treatment, maybe we could get him back to shifting in a blink of an eye like he used to when he was a child.

Do you want a ride? The corner of his mouth quirked up in a funny—but unmistakably Nico—dragon smile.

"Don't drop me," I said. "I don't have the adrenaline of battle to keep me wrapped around you."

Should we make you a saddle? His laugh rumbled through me.

"Maybe!" I said. "Riding bareback is hard, and it'd probably be more comfortable for you if I wasn't squeezing the life out of you."

His eyes slanted in what I assumed was a flirty dragon expression. *You can ride me bareback anytime you want.*

I giggled and patted his back. "Okay, lover boy. Crouch down so I can get on."

He flattened himself to the ground, and I hiked my leg over the side of his back. I situated myself on top of him and laid my chest on his back, wrapping my arms around his neck and squeezing my thigh muscles to stay on. It wasn't all that bad actually; he was wide enough that I didn't have to balance. My handhold was securely wrapped around his neck.

Ready?

"Yes!"

He unfolded his wings. The thin membranes glimmered in the sunlight. His flapping rustled the grasses below us as he sprang into the air. My shrill scream escaped even though I'd been braced for the moment the air caught under his wings.

I forced my eyes open and took in the green landscape of the forest under us. Nico flew out to the coast, and we dove toward the ocean. The droplets of cool salt water sprayed on my face.

A happy dragon roar rumbled through his body, through mine. He soared high into the sky. His corded muscles undulated under my thighs.

Our bond sparkled and thrummed between us. We didn't need words. A simple, divine happiness radiated from him, from his aura. The instinctual place that Nico described himself falling into while being a dragon.

Maybe we would get a saddle. I wanted to sit up, to put my arms out and feel the air the way he felt it under his wings.

But even wrapped tight around him I could experience the thrill and the freedom of flight.

Nico banked left and right through the mountains in the forest, over the meadows and fields and streams. The sun kissed my skin, warm enough that the chill of the air was a relief. Nico flew us around the Molbridge forests until he sensed that my limbs had started to ache from holding on.

We landed back in the meadow at the cabin with a hard thud, the ground and trees shaking and trembling like an avalanche.

A joyful exhilaration enlivened every fiber of my being. The vibration tingled me from my scalp to my toes.

"That was..." Incredible. Magnificent. Indescribable.

I slid off his back and ran to his face, holding his scaley jaw in my hands. "I have no words. Nothing comes close."

I shivered. His excitement and joy were flowing through me and mine to him in turn. We were like one person. One magical being of ethereal lightness. "I feel so…"

He rumbled a growl and nosed my torso, my chest.

I know exactly how you feel.

His nostrils flared and released a curl of smoke. The faint smell of campfire and sweet berries coated my throat. The excitement moved from a high-pitch joy into something lower, something pulsating. A deep bassline had been plucked inside of me.

I exhaled, long and slow, as need throbbed between my legs.

His eyes glimmered with mischief, and his tail slashed back and forth before wrapping around my waist and pulling me close. *Come here, my sweet mate, my fire, my heart.*

THE END

Author Note

I knew when Nico came galloping into the picture, I'd have to write his happily ever after with Sloane. I hope you enjoyed reading these little vignettes and getting a glimpse into their love story.

The Dark Perception Series is officially over. There are three to five standalone books planned for the spinoff series. We will be back in Palagui and Delnee, following characters you've already been introduced to (Yes, Gwen and Daria will get a book!). The vibe of the spinoff series may feel a little different than what you've read so far. Amaya's story was written as a reflection of my own mental health journey, which, as you can imagine, made the story very personal. You can be assured though that there will continue to be magic, smut, emotional relationships, and mental health representation.

Join my author release newsletter & I'll send you two exclusive free novellas. Sign up on my website at AlexandraLarson.com/freebie.

Leaving a review on Amazon is the best way to help indie authors. If you'd like to support my work, please consider leaving a review! Don't have time? No worries—even just a star rating helps immensely.

Tandem Reread

*Note: I would not recommend reading *My Fire My Heart* without finishing the first three books, as there are major spoilers.

Ascend from the Shadows Chapters 1-19
Chapter One: The Hopeless Romantic
Chapter Two: The Free Spirit
Ascend from the Shadows Chapters 20-24
Chapter Three: The Flames
Chapter Four: The Irony
Finish Ascend & Read Descend into the Void Chapters 1-7
Chapter Five: The Dragon
Descend into the Void Chapter 8
Chapter Six: The Bargain
Descend into the Void Chapter 9
Chapter Seven: The Flirt
Chapter Eight: The Itch
Chapter Nine: The Light
Chapter Ten: The Flashback
Chapter Eleven: The Move
Descend into the Void Chapters 10
Chapter Twelve: The Fake Out
Descend into the Void Chapters 11-12
Chapter Thirteen: The Redo
Descend into the Void Chapters 13-14
Chapter Fourteen: The Healing
Descend into the Void Chapter 15-16
Chapter Fifteen: The Partial Truth
Descend into the Void 17-19
Chapter Sixteen: The Cave
Chapter Seventeen: The Toys

Chapter Eighteen: The Next Morning
Descend into the Void Chapters 20-24
Chapter Nineteen: The Betrayal
Descend into the Void 25-31
Chapter Twenty: The Ghosting
Finish Descend into the Void
Chapter Twenty-One: The Declaration
Chapter Twenty-Two: The Reconciliation
Chapter Twenty-Three: The True Form
Seize the Power Chapters 1-7
Chapter Twenty-Four: The Bond
Seize the Power Chapters 8-32
Chapter Twenty-Five: The Power to Heal
Finish Seize the Power
Chapter Twenty-Six: The Future
Epilogue: The Dragon

Playlist

Cool for the Summer – Demi Lovato (Sloane's Song)

Tear in My Heart – Twenty One Pilots (Nico's Song)

Symphony – Sawyer Hill (Chapter 5: The Dragon)

Fire – Barn Courtney (Chapter 6: The Bargain)

New Girl – FINNEAS (Chapter 7: The Flirt)

Love Me Harder – Steven Rodriguez (Chapter 8: The Itch)

Feel Right Now – Sawyer Hill (Chapter 9: The Light)

Sunshine of Your Love – Cream (Chapter 11: The Move)

Holy Water – Bad Company (Chapter 15: The Partial Truth)

Hard to Handle – The Black Crowes (Chapter 16: The Cave)

Feel Like Makin' Love – Bad Company (Chapter 17: The Toys)

Burnin' For You – Blue Oyster Cult (Chapter 18: The Next Morning)

Piece of My Heart – Janis Joplin (Chapter 19: The Betrayal)

Hell's Comin' With Me – Poor Man's Poison (Chapter 20: The Ghosting)

Hearts Burst into Fire – Bullet for My Valentine (Chapter 21: The Declaration)

Fire – Black Honey (Chapter 22: The Reconciliation)

Gold Dandelions – Barns Courtney (Chapter 24: The Bond)

Midlife Crisis – House Parties (Chapter 25: The Power to Heal)

Hellfire – Barns Courtney (Battle in Seize the Power)

Never Let You Down – Barns Courtney (Chapter 26: The Future & Epilogue: The Dragon)

Summer '92 – Black Honey (Vibes)

Barns Courtney – The Attractions of Youth Album (Vibes)

Spotify & YouTube playlist links can be found on my website.
AlexandraLarson.com

About the Author

Alexandra Larson is a business woman by day and romance author by night. When she's not writing or reading, she's trying to soak up the limited amount of sun the Northern Hemisphere provides.

Sign up for her author newsletter to be the first to know about new releases at AlexandraLarson.com/newsletter.